Stories by Contemporary Writers from Shanghai

CALLING BACK THE SPIRIT OF THE DEAD

T0095716

This book is edited and designed by the Editorial Committee of *Cultural China* series

Text by Peng Ruigao
Translation by Yawtsong Lee
Cover Image by Quanjing
Interior Design by Xue Wenqing
Cover Design by Wang Wei

Assistant Editor: Hou Weiting
Editors: Yang Xinci, Nina Train Choa
Editorial Director: Zhang Yicong

Senior Consultants: Sun Yong, Wu Ying, Yang Xinci
Managing Director and Publisher: Wang Youbu

ISBN: 978-1-60220-241-2

Address any comments about *Calling Back the Spirit of the Dead* to:

Better Link Press
99 Park Ave
New York, NY 10016
USA

or

Shanghai Press and Publishing Development Company
F 7 Donghu Road, Shanghai, China (200031)
Email: comments_betterlinkpress@hotmail.com

Printed in China by Shanghai Donnelley Printing Co., Ltd.

1   3   5   7   9   10   8   6   4   2

CALLING BACK
THE SPIRIT
OF THE DEAD

By Peng Ruigao

Better Link Press

Foreword

This collection of books for English readers consists of short stories and novellas published by writers based in Shanghai. Apart from a few who are immigrants to Shanghai, most of them were born in the city, from the latter part of the 1940s to the 1980s. Some of them had their works published in the late 1970s and the early 1980s; some gained recognition only in the 21st century. The older among them were the focus of the "To the Mountains and Villages" campaign in their youth, and as a result, lived and worked in the villages. The difficult paths of their lives had given them unique experiences and perspectives prior to their eventual return to Shanghai. They took up creative writing for different reasons but all share a creative urge and a love for writing. By profession, some of them are college professors, some literary editors, some directors of literary institutions, some freelance writers and some professional writers. From the individual styles of the authors and the art of their writings, readers can easily detect traces of the authors' own experiences in life, their interests, as well as their aesthetic values. Most of the works in this collection are still written in the realistic style that represents, in a painstakingly fashioned fictional world, the changes of the times in urban and rural life. Having grown up in a more open era, the younger writers have been spared the hardships experienced by their predecessors, and therefore seek greater freedom in their writing. Whatever category of writers they belong to, all of them have gained their rightful places in the Chinese literary circles over the last forty years. Shanghai writers tend to favor urban narratives more than other genres of writing. Most of the works in this collection can be characterized as urban literature with Shanghai characteristics, but there are also exceptions.

Called the "Paris of the East," Shanghai was already an international metropolis in the 1920s and 30s. Being the center of China's economy, culture and literature at the time, it housed a majority of writers of importance in the history of modern Chinese literature. The list includes Lu Xun, Guo Moruo, Mao Dun and Ba Jin, who had all written and published prolifically in Shanghai. Now, with Shanghai re-emerging as a globalized metropolis, the Shanghai writers who have appeared on the literary scene in the last forty years all face new challenges and literary quests of the times. I am confident that some of the older writers will produce new masterpieces. As for the fledging new generation of writers, we naturally expect them to go far in their long writing careers ahead of them. In due course, we will also introduce those writers who did not make it into this collection.

Wang Jiren
Series Editor

Contents

Calling Back the Spirit of the Dead

1

It caught everyone in our compound by surprise; it had such a profound impact on me that it changed my behavior for a time and caused my hair to turn almost completely gray in the short space of six months.

It happened on April 21, in mid-spring, which fell on the day of grain rain in the solar term of the Chinese lunar calendar. It had not been called the day of grain rain inaccurately, for it did rain that day.

The solar term has become increasingly senseless to modern society. I'll bet out of every one hundred young people in the street no more than one could recite the twenty-four nodes and midpoints of the solar terms. Few of the cadres in the compound of our Tacheng town government had a clue what the solar terms meant.

But I can truthfully say that Wei Shouyi and I— we were Deputy Town Chiefs—were well versed in the solar terms. After all, our livelihood depended on it. Wei Shouyi was the Deputy Town Chief responsible for crops and livestock, which are closely related to the solar terms. Although put in charge of education and culture, I had been given the additional responsibility of overseeing the science and technology station, which had some intersection with solar terms also. Wei Shouyi and I shared an office, in which our desks stood back to back, and we even shared a telephone. As far as we were concerned, no matter how the world evolved outside, one thing never changed in our little corner of the world and that was the solar terms.

Late that night the town office secretary, Little Ye came to knock on my door. He cried, panting heavily, "Chief Peng! The Big Man wants you in the town office, now!"

When I turned on the light and saw that it was barely two in the morning, I took Little Ye to task. "Is something wrong with you? Why are you howling at this ungodly hour?"

Little Ye said timidly, "What am I supposed to do? The Big Man and Party Secretary Shang are waiting for you in the town office."

I threw some clothes on, took the bicycle parked under the staircase and pedaled quickly in the rain toward the town government compound.

It was raining hard. The cold rain hitting my warm body caused me to wince and shiver. When I passed the few dim roadside lamps, I could feel steam rising from the roots of my hair. The world was still in slumber and the small town's streets were deserted. There was only the vexing sound of the steady downpour, falling in dense, fine sheets.

On the way I asked Little Ye again, "What goddamn business is so urgent that you had to come to my home so late in the night and holler like you were trying to catch a thief?"

Again he professed his ignorance. "I just roused the Big Man from bed too. Party Secretary Shang is the one on duty tonight. Only he knows what's going on; Party Secretary Shang called for the Big Man, and the Big Man asked for you."

The Big Man, You Baida, was Town Chief of Tacheng. He was called the Big Man because, first of all, his name contains the character *da*, which means big, and second because the cadres in the town government compound have a habit of calling their town chief "the Big Man." It's as if the town government compound was a ferry, and the town chief—the Big Man—was piloting the boat, and the rest of us were passengers in the same boat, rising and falling with it—so fittingly.

When I rushed into the Party Secretary's office, it was already filled with smoke. Party Secretary Shang and the Big Man, two chain smokers sitting across from each other, were pulling on their cigarettes in silence. The ashtray on the desk was piled high with cigarette butts, looking like a crud of dog turd.

The Big Man waved at me and motioned me to a chair. He had a hangdog, grouchy, persecuted look, his eyes bloodshot, apparently from being roused in mid-sleep. His bristly crew cut, which normally gave him an air of authority, looked unkempt now, suddenly making our town chief, who was barely over fifty, look much older than his age.

Party Secretary Shang said, "Town Chief Peng, unexpected things can and do happen. A grave matter came up in our town government and I want to exchange ideas with you about it."

I asked, suddenly alarmed, "What is the matter?"

Party Secretary Shang cast a glance at the Big Man before saying, "Big Man! Tell him what happened."

Party Secretary resumed smoking, deliberately turning his face away from the Big Man and me. I couldn't understand why.

The Big Man threw a cigarette to me and, when he saw me light it up, said abruptly, "Ah Peng, Shouyi is dead."

I was so startled I bumped my lighter into the tip of my cigarette, sending off sparks.

I said, "No. You must be kidding?"

Turning his head back to face us, Party Secretary Shang said to me with a grave expression, "We are in an official meeting! Would we joke about such things?"

"But Shouyi was fine this afternoon," I said. "How could he die just like that?"

"He died in an auto accident. The county police just notified us," said the Big Man.

Party Secretary Shang suddenly stamped his foot on the ground and said with gnashed teeth, "It's all the fault of that car!"

After vehemently denouncing the car he shook his head emphatically. All the cadres in the compound would have known what he meant by that.

Following his appointment as Deputy Town Chief, Wei Shouyi made it his first priority to learn how to drive. The normal fee charged for learning to drive was in the neighborhood of four or five thousand yuan, but he was able to get into the driving program without paying a dime because he had connections. On the first day of the course, he said to me, "Going forward cadres must all learn a few skills. First: using the computer, and second: driving a car ..."

I completed his enumeration with, "Third: dancing; fourth: dating girls." And both of us laughed.

Wei Shouyi resumed his serious tone, saying, "Learning to drive is really very important. It will make conducting official business as well as personal affairs so much more efficient. In the future when you, Town Chief Peng, need a car, you no longer have to apply to the town office for it; I have no patience with those snobbish bastards. In the future I, Wei Shouyi, will drive you, to Suzhou, Shanghai, wherever you want to go."

"That's too kind of you," I quickly replied. "But I wouldn't have the impudence to have a town chief chauffeur me around."

After Wei Shouyi got his driver's license, he looked everywhere for a car to drive. The town government had acquired a few cars in recent years, but they couldn't let Wei Shouyi drive any of them. Big Man and Party Secretary Shang shared an Audi, but other cadres in the deputy category in the town government

were denied permission. Two other smaller cars were
both very old Santana 2000s. Deputy Town Chiefs
and Deputy Party Secretaries could not automatically
get permission to drive even these almost vintage cars,
because they were assigned by the office according to
the importance of the purpose they were used for. Wei
Shouyi said, "I wouldn't take these jalopies even if
they made a gift of them to me; I don't want to trouble
the town office." He borrowed cars from enterprises
and businesses run by the town government for up to
two weeks, even ten days at a time. He got to drive
cars of different colors, but mostly from the Santana
line. Wei Shouyi's borrowing from town enterprises
was frowned upon by Party Secretary Shang, but the
Big Man said, "Well, the town government is not
procuring any additional cars, so if he can borrow
cars to drive, we shouldn't stop him." So, the town
government winked at Deputy Town Chief Wei and
did not interfere with it.

The car driven by Wei Shouyi that day had been
borrowed from Galloping Horses Real Developers,
Inc.

Galloping Horses was the fastest growing
enterprise in our town in the past few years, due
mainly to its ability to seize opportunities in the real

estate market in a timely fashion. From the town government it received permits to develop prime real estate, and at advantageous land prices. Soon Galloping Horses was raking in huge profits. Wang Shuangxi, owner of Galloping Horses, grew up in the same village as Wei Shouyi and was once a colleague of his in the town government. They were thick as thieves. For many years, one of them would work to speed up the approval process in the town bureaucracy and the other would build and sell apartments on the construction sites. It was a well-oiled well-coordinated collaboration. Before setting up the real estate business, Wang Shuangxi was manager of the Tacheng Stock Farm; he had the nickname "swine expert." The town government owned a large share of Galloping Horses Real Developers, Inc.

Wang Shuangxi was an ambitious businessman. He liked to say, "Why did I name the company Galloping Horses? Because I aim to build housing— and quality housing at that—at a galloping pace, and build the town of Tacheng into a small city where everybody enjoys a decent standard of living." He got rich quickly as a real estate developer. Soon he built himself a three-story house topped by a big satellite dish that enabled him to watch TV programs from abroad. He reportedly had bought an apartment in Shanghai, where a young woman waited at his pleasure. Wei Shouyi borrowed a car from him and kept it for a long time. Wang Shuangxi did not mind; he drove a Benz, a black S500. His vice presidents got to drive the "Crown," a Japanese make. So lending a Passat to Wei Shouyi was not a big deal. As Galloping Horses prospered, the cadres in the town government were generously provided for. On days of festivities and every so often, Galloping Horses would issue all kinds of bonuses—service bonus or special festivity bonus, to name a few—to the town officials. Lower-level cadres received anywhere from three thousand to five thousand yuan, and the town chief and deputy chiefs pocketed upwards of ten thousand. The bonuses made everyone happy, although they would say tauntingly, "Who'd have thought that Wang Shuangxi the swine expert would one day turn into a real estate expert, and an expert at passing out bonuses ..."

I asked the two bosses, "Should we notify Wang Shuangxi about the auto accident involving Town Chief Wei? After all, the car was borrowed from him."

The Town Chief—the Big Man—said, "What's the goddamn point? There was a death. What's a car compared to that?"

Party Secretary Shang said, "We'll keep it to ourselves for now and try as much as possible not to leak the news whether in our town or out of town. There could be serious repercussions."

He paused to draw on his cigarette before continuing. "You, Town Chief Peng, will be responsible today and tomorrow for going to the county government and taking care of the auto accident with the traffic police there."

"There is a meeting tomorrow at the town clinic to discuss the question of births in violation of family planning regulations," I said.

The Big Man said impatiently, "It will be no great loss if you miss that goddamn meeting. Tell your assistant to attend on your behalf. The top priority is a smooth, satisfactory handling of the incident involving Shouyi."

"That's true," agreed Party Secretary Shang.

The Big Man said, "After a little discussion, Party Secretary Shang and I agreed that you are the right person to handle the matter, Town Chief Peng. You represent the town party organization and you and Shouyi were good friends."

Party Secretary Shang cast a quick but significant

glance at me.

I asked, "Will Shouyi's family come along with me tomorrow to the county to participate in the discussion?"

Shooting a glance at Party Secretary Shang, the Big Man said, "Party Secretary Shang and I have been scratching our heads about this. We have not yet notified Qin Dujuan about Shouyi's accident."

Qin Dujuan, Wei Shouyi's wife, was a teacher at the town middle school.

The Big Man continued, "No need to look elsewhere for someone to do this. Why don't you, Town Chief Peng, take up this task as well?"

I quickly shook my head. If it were any other woman that I was assigned to deal with, I would not have hesitated to do it, but not Qin Dujuan. There was this thing that happened between that woman and me, and since that thing I had resolved not to see her ever again.

I said, "I'd better concentrate on going to the county and taking care of the matter of the traffic accident. As for talking to Qin Dujuan, you two are more suitable for the job. You are the heads of our town; and it's better that you deal with a matter of such gravity."

Party Secretary Shang, again, cast a meaningful glance at me and nodded all right. "Town Chief Peng has a point there."

The Big Man yawned and lit another cigarette. "First thing tomorrow morning you take my Audi to the county. Don't forget to bring two cartons of choice cigarettes. Do you know anybody in the traffic police?"

I nodded, remembering Qiu Sanbao. He and I were roommates when we boarded at the county middle school; he slept in the bunk below me. He worked now in the traffic police brigade.

The Big Man said, "You must know someone. If you don't, then find one I don't care how. Traffic incidents are nothing to sneeze at. The determination of the liability and how the final report is written will affect his funeral arrangements and other posthumous affairs to a great degree. Do you understand?"

I said I did.

The Big Man studied me for a moment, got to his feet abruptly and started shaking his head. As his eyes reddened around the rims, he said, "Wei Shouyi, oh, Wei Shouyi! What rotten luck you got! You had everything going for you—a college diploma, great qualities, a promising career, you name it. And the next moment you are gone! Go figure!"

Party Secretary Shang kept sighing. The Big Man's eyes were now furiously red and big teardrops cascaded down over his visibly swelling eyes. I could almost hear the tears fall. I was seeing tears in the Big Man's eyes for the first time since I started working in the town government.

"He was thirty-seven, what, thirty-eight?" said the Big Man. "In the prime of his life. A few more years of honing his skills on the job and Wei Shouyi, would no doubt have taken the helm of Tacheng. He was dealt a really lousy hand."

Party Secretary Shang again glanced at me. That night all his glances seemed fraught with meaning.

The Big Man wiped away his tears, not, as most people do, with the back of his hand, or a finger, but in this unique way of scraping off his tears, with the heel of his thumb, in an upward motion from the eye bags. This had the effect of further blurring and smearing his eyes, instead of clearing away the tears. The wings of his nose flared. Clearly the Big Man's grief was genuine.

And it was little wonder. Everybody in the compound knew that Wei Shouyi had been personally groomed by the Big Man as his eventual successor ...

The tear-streaked Big Man continued. "Our Shouyi was smart. His 'introduction of vegetables from abroad' was a huge success. When most people in our country won't touch farming with a ten-foot pole nowadays, our Shouyi was undaunted and he really enjoyed farming and made a name for himself doing it. He even won acclaim from professors at the Academy of Agricultural Sciences. There aren't many capable people like him in our town or even in our county!"

His eyes closed, Party Secretary Shang continued to shake his head.

The Big Man said with tears in his eyes, "Well it can't be helped if it's his karma to have a short life. Only what a pity it is for Qin Dujuan! It will be tough on her. Anyway whatever it takes we have to give him a grand funeral that will comfort the living and honor the dead ..."

Outside, the rain was pouring down with a vengeance. It was a cold night and the damp, cold wind blowing in through the cracks in the door was bone chilling, causing us to shiver involuntarily.

As I listened to the fond reminiscences of the Big Man and Party Secretary Shang about Wei Shouyi, my eyes too began to moisten.

The unexpected death of Wei Shouyi felt like a dream; it was hard to believe and to accept. I'd sat across from him at the same desk in our office for so many years I'd lost count. When people talked about the young and upcoming generation in the Tacheng town bureaucracy, two names came up by far the most; one was Wei Shouyi and the other was mine. We would often appear together at many functions. We were in the same age bracket, shared similar experiences and even looked alike. Only, Wei Shouyi was more capable, more resourceful and more well known in every respect. Of particular note was the effort he put into the research and planting of eco-friendly vegetables, which resulted in Tacheng Township becoming a major center of eco-friendly vegetable production and winning wide praise from the county and city authorities. In that, he set a hopelessly high bar for me. There was inevitable friction and tension between us at the workplace, but deep down inside there was mutual respect. Frankly, I didn't need the persuasion of the Big Man and Party Secretary; I would have done my level best to speak for Wei Shouyi's interests, for old times' sake if for nothing else, especially at a moment like this.

Town Chief You nodded at me, teary-eyed, and

repeatedly said, "Ah Peng, thank you for undertaking this tough task, thank you."

Party Secretary Shang chimed in. "Town Chief Peng is the best man for the job. We trust you. There's no better candidate. Ah Peng, when you're in the county government office, keep your cool; listen to what people have to say but don't volunteer any comments; make sure you know exactly how to proceed before taking action. Play it by ear, but if any problem arises, be sure to seek instructions from Town Chief You."

You Baida interjected, "And be sure to report what's going on to Party Secretary Shang."

Their instructions put me in a dilemma. Who should I report to or seek instructions from when I needed to make a decision? I lifted my eyes to watch the two hands of the electric clock move jerkily ahead and gave an ambiguous reply. "I will telephone."

The Big Man looked at his watch and said, "Daybreak is still two or three hours away. Ah Peng, why don't you go get some sleep in your office? You will have to leave early for the county government office and you'll have a busy day ahead. Party Secretary Shang and I will talk some more about how to break the news to Qin Dujuan."

I said all right and got up and left.

I made my way toward my office through the unlit corridor, surrounded by pitch darkness; the rain came down in noisy torrents, and I could feel fine sprays of rain on my face; gusts of cold wind obstructed by the wall whirled about me. I fumbled for the key and felt in the dark for the keyhole. My hand trembling, I was for a time unable to insert the key into the keyhole. I was gripped by an oppressive sense of dread in the dark, surrounded by the sounds of rain and wind.

I paused with a hand on the door, thinking: this was the door Wei Shouyi used to open; this was where he took out his key every day. I knew so well that key ring of his: It always hung by a stainless steel chain from his waist, never leaving him for a moment. The ring held all his essential keys. He said once that his life and property depended on it. On the key ring was a small, delicate private seal-chop carved out of ivory; it was a thin, narrow, rectangular slab on which were inscribed the three characters, Wei—Shou—Yi, of his name in official script. When the wages came from the treasurer's office, he would bring out this private seal hanging on his waist and stamp it on the document as his signature. The three raised characters on the chop's end were tiny but finely detailed. Everybody in the town government compound marveled at the fine craftsmanship of the chop; he truly cherished it and was often observed taking it out when he got a moment to admire it with squinted eyes ...

After unlocking and opening the door, I was engulfed in a darker obscurity. Feeling the wall with my hand I found the damp, cold switch. With a click, I threw the switch up; a shrill hiss rose from the florescent lamp and the light came on after some flickering, inadequately illuminating the walls. The first thing that sprang into my sight in the pale, anemic light was not my own chair but Wei Shouyi's desk.

In his haste to depart that afternoon Wei Shouyi had left his chair at an angle to the desk and the towel draped on the chair back was still damp; on the glass top of the desk lay the previous night's county newspaper. I knew that the first page of the paper featured a report about him entitled "The Number One Vegetable Farmer of the County," which gave an account of how he had pioneered the introduction of a variety of vegetables from abroad. I saw how Wei Shouyi's eyes shone and his face brightened up when he received that copy of the county newspaper; he read and reread the article in a rapt state of absorption, giving an occasional chuckle. He asked me to read the article. When I skimmed through it, saying, "Hmm, well written! It's about time a journalist wrote you up!" I was feeling something entirely different from what I was saying. My relationship with Wei Shouyi was not always what it seemed to people ...

I stood in a corner of the office, my eyes resting on that county paper and Wei Shouyi's desk for a long while, feeling lost and empty.

In the office, where the windows were kept tightly closed, a familiar smoky odor, left by Wei Shouyi's cigarettes, lingered in the air. I preferred tea and had never smoked; I was therefore particularly sensitive to the smell of cigarette smoke. Wei Shouyi liked a brand of ginseng cigarettes made in northeast China. That was more to my taste. I'd always been fascinated by the way he held his cigarette, with his middle and index fingers stretched straight and the other three fingers tucked away, almost invisible, striking a pose that bespoke manly vigor and decisiveness. He also had an elegant way of blowing out smoke: he would smack his lips, as if savoring the flavor, half close his eyes and blow out the smoke in a long exhalation, with an air of genteel rapture. The scent of that particular brand of cigarettes grew on me; you really could detect an aroma of ginseng in the smoky haze—it was so subtle that it was discernible only if you consciously sniffed for it but would otherwise smelled like the silk of overripe corn. It was an urbane, mild but stubborn smell, so fine that it insinuated itself into the cracks and crannies in the walls, into the desks and cabinets, and into the piles of documents and newspapers, and then spread slowly to suffuse the air, becoming the signature smell of this office ... The smell reminded me of the grotesque way Wei Shouyi had of fixing his eyes on the tip of his nose whenever he lit up his cigarette and of how his face became blurred by the haze of smoke. I sniffed the air, flaring my nostrils, as if anxious that the smell might dissipate. A whisper rose from the depth of my heart: Shouyi, Wei Shouyi! You left in such a hurry!

It was a white night for me.

2

It was my first meeting in several years with Qiu Sanbao, the traffic policeman, who had apparently advanced in his career, and was exuding a busy, capable air.

He said, "It's too chaotic here. Let's talk in the lounge."

We were talking in the office of the Traffic Incidents Unit. Indeed it was a chaotic scene, with sputum, cigarette butts and litter strewn everywhere, and the loud arguing, cursing and crying of those responsible for the accidents and the victims' parties.

On the way to the police lounge, Qiu Sanbao said, "I knew you'd be sent here to deal with the Wei Shouyi incident."

I asked, "How did you know?"

Qiu Sanbao said, "Here in the county government everybody knows you and Wei Shouyi are the left and right legs of Tacheng Town."

I made no comment on that but only asked, "Where is Wei Shouyi now?"

Qiu Sanbao gestured at a one-story building visible from the window. "He is on ice in that building."

Looking at the gray cement building, the closed iron gate, and hearing the word "ice" coming out of his mouth, I felt a chill in my heart.

Qiu Sanbao asked, "Do you want to see him? I'll tell them to open up."

I seemed to hear the clanking of the iron gate

being opened, and to see Wei Shouyi under a white sheet in an icy room that reeked of chemicals and the white sheet lifted to reveal the face of Wei Shouyi that perhaps would no longer be recognized by me ...

I said, "I don't want to trouble them to open the gate. Let's not do it now."

Qiu Sanbao resumed walking with a chuckle. I asked, "Sanbao, how do you think the nature of this incident will be characterized?"

Qiu Sanbao said, "What's to characterize? It's open and shut. It's not as if it involved the collision between two cars or between a person and a car; then you'd have to determine the main responsibility and the secondary. Wei Shouyi drove his car straight into the river and drowned. How else would you characterize it?"

I thought to myself: Qiu Sanbao must have seen and dealt with too many such incidents and which is why he talks about them in a callous manner, without showing any respect for the dead and without any attempt at subtlety. I was a little disconcerted by the way he talked, but I had no choice but to go along perfunctorily. I said, "Yes, I guess that's right."

Qiu Sanbao suddenly paused and suggested in all seriousness, "Why don't you take a look at the scene of the accident? No amount of explanation does a better job of clarifying than an onsite survey. That car hasn't been pulled out of the river yet."

After considering it I said, "I might as well do that."

Qiu Sanbao continued, "I made the suggestion only because you are an old school mate of mine. If I did it for every accident, I'd be exhausted."

I thanked him. Qiu Sanbao took a police car and blew through town like an autumn wind, with siren blaring, and headed toward the scene of the accident.

The spot was near the 12-kilometer mark of the County Road, by a river. I didn't know the name of the river, except that it was very deep at that point and the water was clear. Qiu Sanbao and I stepped off our car. From the distance I saw a cluster of onlookers on the riverbank. Sanbao approached them and shouted with a grim face, "Move aside, move aside!" He went down to the water edge in big strides, with me following close behind.

Someone was heard asking, "Is the family here?"

A silver gray Passat was submerged in the river pointing toward the bottom; a small part of the tail end was above water and remained dry and shiny. Qiu Sanbao sat down on his haunches and said, with

CALLING BACK THE SPIRIT OF THE DEAD   35

a cigarette in his mouth, "The accident was reported by village folk here. But for their report, we wouldn't have found out so soon."

"If the villagers who were first on the scene had got down into the river, Shouyi could perhaps have had a chance of surviving," I said.

Qiu Sanbao said, "No way." The villagers found it late at night when they were laying fishing lines for soft-shell turtles. The guy who discovered the vehicle in the river was so spooked he peed in his pants. When our duty officer received the report he immediately drove down at a breakneck speed. By the time he arrived on the scene, Town Chief Wei had been in the water for two hours.

I asked, "Can you tell how many hours a person has been in the water?"

Qiu Sanbao said, "Our captain is a veteran in these matters. He can tell."

I said, "Did Town Chief Wei drive while intoxicated?"

Qiu Sanbao said, "It is a possibility. We can't say for sure at this time. It'll have to wait until forensic tests are done."

I tried to picture how Wei Shouyi, fired by the alcohol in his veins, sank into the gas pedal, making his car take off like a shot. He enjoyed fast driving. He would have been thrilled by the Passat roaring through the night, the two beams of its bright headlights piercing the nocturnal fog like two arrows ... heaven knows how he drove straight into the river!

I got up and surveyed the surroundings. The County Road was indeed a little on the narrow side, but there were no sharp turns in this part of the road; under normal driving conditions, there was no reason for the car to go off the road and end up in the river. I asked Qiu Sanbao, "Was he speeding? Did he lose control of the car due to high speed?"

Qiu Sanbao drew on his cigarette and looked at the river in silence. The onlookers from the nearby village, realizing from Sanbao's police uniform that we were officials investigating the incident, gathered at our back and listened attentively to our conversation; I could feel puffs of warm breath on the back of my neck.

Qiu Sanbao rose to his feet and said to the villagers, "Disperse, disperse! Stop gawking!"

The villagers dispersed and backed away a bit, but shortly knotted about us again, this time a little farther from us than before. Qiu Sanbao said, "How can we know exactly the speed at which the car was going? The dead man can't tell us that. But judging by the tire marks on the sand banks, I'm quite certain the car was going very fast."

I followed Qiu Sanbao's pointing finger. The exposed sandbank lay below the roadbed, separated from the latter by a barren stretch of land about ten feet wide. The car apparently left the road at a great speed, gouged a pit the size of a vat in the barrens, plowed up a swath of mud and weeds before plunging into the river. Wei Shouyi's death almost appeared preordained: The road was densely lined with trees whose trunks were as thick as a cow's thigh; any one of them could have blocked the hurtling car but none did. If he had crashed his car into a tree, there could have been a different outcome.

I asked, "Who got Town Chief Wei's body out of the water last night?"

Qiu Sanbao said, "Who else? I got into the water myself."

I looked at him.

Sanbao said. "He needn't have died. When I dived into the water I could tell by feeling with my hands that the car windows were open and the door was not damaged. When the water started pouring in he could with some agility have climbed out of a window quickly and survived. But he didn't; instead he remained seated with the seatbelt buckled!"

Suddenly something occurred to me: could it be that in a moment of panic Wei Shouyi was unable to free himself from the seat belt and thus drowned in his seat?

Qiu Sanbao said, "Town Chief Peng! Don't even mention a scenario like that! Our traffic laws require wearing a seat belt. If word were to spread that Wei Shouyi's death had anything to do with the seat belt, it would make it more difficult for us to enforce the law."

I said, "I was just confidentially exploring the possibilities with you, Sanbao; it was just for our ears."

Sanbao said, "I was considering another scenario: Is it possible that when the car plunged off the road, then hurtled across the sandbank, the successive shocks knocked Wei Shouyi unconscious? Or perhaps the sudden loss of control of his speeding car paralyzed him with terror? How else would you explain the fact that a smart and resourceful man like Wei Shouyi did not know how to escape with his life when the possibility was there?"

I nodded, "You may be right. It's a plausible scenario."

A villager asked clumsily, "You're just letting the car soak in the river? Aren't the authorities going to hoist it out of the water?"

Sanbao gave him a sharp look, "So kind of you to be concerned. You think it's easy to get it out of the water, eh?"

The villager said, "I'll come back with two tractors and we will haul it out of the river in no time, I promise."

Sanbao said, "So you'll pay for the use of the tractors? And you will also get into the water to hook up the steel cable, I'm sure?"

The villager fell silent. Sanbao turned to me and said, "A tow truck has been called, but it's not available yet. A run of bad luck! Too many accidents recently!"

On the way back to the county office, I placed two cartons of "Zhonghua" cigarettes on the back seat. Qiu Sanbao saw them and did not put up a show of refusing the gift. I relayed the town government's wishes and requested Sanbao's help in determining the nature and liabilities of the accident. Sanbao said, "This accident involved only one car and no other person than the deceased, so it shouldn't be difficult to accommodate your wishes."

That put my mind at ease.

Back at the office of the traffic police brigade, Sanbao again took me to the lounge and told me to wait. About ten minutes later, he came back, followed by a policewoman. He said, "There are some personal effects left behind by the deceased Wei Shouyi; you can sign for them and take them back with you."

At the mention of the personal effects left behind by the deceased my hairs bristled. I looked blankly at the policewoman, trying to imagine what she would produce. The policewoman opened the flap of a big envelope, turned it upside down and emptied the contents on the desk.

A key ring, a cell phone, a wallet, a fountain pen, a lighter, a watch … all so familiar because I had seen them every day!

The policewoman opened the flap of a smaller envelope and emptied it: a half pack of Ginseng brand cigarettes fell with a plop on the desk.

Sanbao observed casually, "What good are these cigarettes now? They are all soggy."

The policewoman said, "I don't care if they aren't any good. I have to turn over everything that belonged to the deceased." Then she said to me, "There's cash in the wallet. Please count it."

The coldness of her tone reminded me of the

water of the river that drowned Wei Shouyi.

When I picked up the wallet, I felt a bone-chilling coldness at the tip of my fingers. A funny mixture of the stench of the river water and the smell of paper bills arose out of the open wallet; I carefully peeled off the soaked bills that stuck together one at a time with a fingernail, and counted them. The cash came to 1,680 yuan.

Qiu Sanbao said, "1,680! That's a lucky combination of numbers. It should have guarded him against an untimely death!" The policewoman gave a chuckle, picked up the receipt I signed and left. After a while Qiu Sanbao said he had to attend an accident adjudication meeting and left also.

I was left alone with the pile of Wei Shouyi's stuff in the now deserted policemen's lounge. It was quiet indoors and out. The lounge was located in a corner of the traffic police building, separated from the urban hustle and bustle by a plaza, which was enlivened only by swarms of chattering sparrows flying over and descending on it. Occasional whiffs of frying oil accompanied by the clanking of metal turners against steel woks came out of the kitchen.

I sat there for a long time. When I casually picked up his cell phone and flipped it open, a drop of ice-cold water fell onto my knee. I remembered how Wei Shouyi used to make cell phone calls. He would first go to an open space; he'd have one hand on his waist and his head tilted up, as if he were watching an airplane in flight, or he were in conversation with the heavens above. The cell phone was an imported high-end model, that cost thousands of yuan, not normally seen in the hands of town government officials. I was going to have to ask around to find out if it had been a gift from Wang Shuangxi, the owner of Galloping Horses Developers, Inc.

Supposedly a cell phone is no longer useable once water gets into it. Even an imported cell phone, I thought, when in the water for such a long time, would certainly have been damaged beyond salvage. I shook it a few times and wiped the screen clean. Then I pressed the on/off key with an extended finger to see if it indeed was on the fritz. I was surprised when, with a beep, a blue light leapt up from the small screen; so the cell was alive!

For a long time I fixed a blank stare on the small display. This had been Wei Shouyi's most important means of communication. The car and the cell phone had meant a greater amount of work for him, but had also brought him greater pleasure. He often brought out this cell phone in the office and played with it, sometimes for as long as half an hour. At this moment, while that Passat was still lying ice-cold in the river, the cell phone lit up and came to life in the palm of my hand. I involuntarily drew a long breath and my heart did a flip.

I put down the cell phone and looked at the watch, which had also survived the crash. It was not an expensive brand, but an imported Enicar, which kept good time. I compared its time with the time on my watch and was amazed by the exact match. Its second hand moved with firmness and gravity, forging ahead fearlessly, the pace, accompanied by a pleasing tick-tock, evoking the brisk gait of youth; its springiness and rhythm also reminded me of Wei Shouyi's footsteps echoing in our town government compound. As I looked at the watch, I thought to myself: human life is so fragile; as fragile as a bean sprout snapped in half; unlike this watch and this cell phone, which, despite the death of their owner, ran on unaffected, as if endowed with a life of their own.

I was startled out of my reverie by a sudden vibration of that cell phone on the desk; it buzzed and spun on the desk. A shiver ran through me and my hairs bristled with dread. Wei Shouyi must be talking to someone about some important business before the fatal accident and had kept the phone on vibrate so as not to be disturbed. The cell phone spinning on the desk brought memories of Wei Shouyi pacing about in the compound; I felt a tug in my heart.

It was eerie to think that someone was calling a dead man on his phone.

I quickly snatched up the phone, but hesitated to flip it open. The vibration continued, causing a tingling sensation in my palm. Maybe it was my over-sensitive nerves, but I had a sense that the vibration was becoming more urgent. I was thinking fast and furiously: should I or should I not take the call?

I determined I shouldn't take the call, which was surely for Shouyi only. What right did I have to take the call on his behalf? The caller might want to talk to Town Chief Wei about some business; or it could be a cadre of the town or of one of the villages in its jurisdiction, unaware of Wei Shouyi's accident, calling him to give him a report or seek instructions from him; yet another possibility was that it was some family member of his calling.

The phone was still vibrating, ever more urgently and violently. On second thought, I said to myself:

Why can't I take a call for Wei Shouyi? I have taken calls for him countless times in the office. What harm can be done if I do it one more time? Maybe the call was about some important official business, and if I could provide an answer on behalf of Town Chief Wei, I could contribute to the resolution of some major issue; or if it was about some major project proposal, I could also acknowledge it for Town Chief Wei. Town Chief Wei may well have gone, but life had to go on and the development of our town should not be halted.

My mind was made up and I opened the phone cover, inhaled deeply and spoke up, "Hello—"

No sound came from the other end. Only when I held my breath was I able to detect an almost inaudible static—woooooo, sssssss—evoking the picture of satellite signals pulsing across the sky, actively seeking and searching ...

Suddenly I heard, amid the static, a long, long sigh ...

My grip on the phone tightened; I shouted, "Hello, hello!"

There was no response, only silence.

I asked at a higher register, "May I ask who this is?"

There was still no response, not even a sigh now. A while later, I heard the receiver slam down.

I brought the phone down from my ear and stared at it, as if hoping to uncover something with my eyes. The phone gave off two sharp beeps and the words "low battery" leapt onto the screen. I quickly closed the phone cover.

A dead silence descended on the lounge. I could hear my heart beat. I stood up and moved my eyes toward the window, toward the low building outside, toward that gray iron gate, and pictured Wei Shouyi lying in there. I said in my heart: Shouyi, your departure was too sudden. So many people in the town and the county governments don't know yet that you are gone. They still think you are conducting business as usual as deputy town chief, and are busy promoting your eco-friendly vegetables. They would never have guessed that the auto accident in the river by the County Road involved you, and that you are now lying in a freezing morgue, never to get up again!

After I turned off the cell phone, that long, long sigh continued to haunt me like a ghost, buzzing about my ears. I tried to parse the characteristics of the sound to help me determine the origin of the call: Was it from the town government? A village government? The county government? Or from his family? I couldn't tell.

Then I quit thinking about it. After all, a man like Wei Shouyi had so many contacts, so many friends it was well-nigh impossible to sort through all of them, just as it's impractical to expect other people to have a clear idea about all those I come in contact with in my work as deputy town chief for education and culture and in my social life.

3

As soon as I returned to the town government compound that same day and entered the gate I watched out for any unusual signs. When I got out of the car, Old Ding of the gatehouse signaled that there was a registered letter for me. As I signed for it, I asked if anything had happen in the compound that I should know about. Old Ding told me that other than Wang Shuangxi urgently demanding to see the Big Man, not a darn thing had happened.

At the mention of the name Wang Shuangxi, my heart lurched. I asked, "What did he come here for?"

Old Ding said, "Little Ye, the town office

secretary, let on that the real estate development company of Wang Shuangxi has been going downhill. Since the beginning of the year sales at several of his apartment buildings have been sluggish and he's thinking of pulling the plug. Starting next month he'll suspend the distribution of service fees to the cadres of the town government."

I chuckled and thought: so that's what it's about.

With the registered letter in hand, I went straight to the office of Party Secretary Shang. He was not in his office, so I went to the Big Man's office. He was hunched over his desk writing something. The moment I entered his office, he lifted his head and looked fixedly at me, "Back already? How did things go?"

I gave a full account of what happened and made a point of telling him about the trip I had taken with Qiu Sanbao of the traffic police to the scene of the accident to inspect the submerged car. The Big Man was a little taken aback by what I described and became more attentive. To make myself clearer, I drew a rough diagram for him. The Big Man stared at the drawing, shook his head and sighed. With the heel of his thumb he wiped off tears in an upward motion.

I asked, "Where is Party Secretary Shang?"

The Big Man said that he had at first wanted

him to come to see Qin Dujuan, but after some discussion, they concluded that try as they might, it was impossible to keep the matter from the county government. So Party Secretary Shang took a car and went to brief the county party committee.

I asked, "Then you have not yet paid a visit to Qin Dujuan?"

The Big Man said, "Before he left, Party Secretary Shang left instructions that if he was still not back by noontime, you and I should go together to see Qin Dujuan."

I answered that I needed to tidy up the report on my morning mission to the county government and suggested he go alone.

The Big Man said, "I knew that you would try to wriggle out of this. What's eating you? That thing between you and Qin Dujuan is no big deal. Why are you so uptight about it?"

I kept repeating, "It's a bad idea! It's a bad idea!" and adamantly refused to go with him.

The Big Man suggested we trade tasks, "You finish writing this thing I've started and I'll go alone to see Qin Dujuan. What do you think?"

I asked him what he had been writing.

The Big Man answered, "We need to plan

arrangements concerning Town Chief Wei, don't we? And the eulogy needs to be written, right?"

I reminded him that the accident was still being investigated, "Isn't it a little early to think of these things?" I asked.

The Big Man pulled a somber face, "We have no control over the outcome of the accident investigation; paying tribute to Shouyi, on the other hand, is an important event for us. Once it is decided, we have to implement it without delay. We can't have a situation where we act like headless flies darting blindly about. It's generally a good policy to be prepare early rather than late."

I said, "You have a point."

The Big Man continued, "It's agreed then. Why don't you write Shouyi's eulogy?"

"I'll write it if you insist, but you guys have to vet it." I answered.

The Big Man said, "Very well. I want to emphasize one point: now that Shouyi is dead, it won't hurt for the town government to go out of its way to burnish his legacy."

I said, "I know."

The Big Man answered, "We are all party members, so we know how important the posthumous appraisal is. Frankly Town Chief Wei already kicked the bucket, so he wouldn't know if the eulogy was in more, or less glowing terms. It is for the consumption of the living, especially of Wei Shouyi's family. Do you understand?"

I said I understood.

The Big Man continued, "When the coffin is nailed shut, the final moment comes. No harm's done if we puff up his legacy a little. What do you say?"

I said, "Puff it up? You sure that's a good idea? I'll tell you what I think: When you write the appraisal for the party's records, it's not a good idea to over exaggerate. Better stick close to the reality. What if there is grumbling against the exaggeration? It will not be in the interest of Town Chief Wei or his kin."

The Big Man said, "Hey, Ah Peng! You are so thick! If we don't give him a lift now, there'll be no other opportunity. Who's going to grudge him a little padding, a little lifting at a time like this? You know Chinese show special deference to the dead and value posthumous glorification. If a person has the bad luck to die, what's wrong with putting in a few good words for him? You've attended memorial services and have heard all those invariably florid eulogies. There were those officials who were wined and dined lavishly, or traveled abroad on public funds, or kept mistresses or had their hand in the public till, but did you hear any of it mentioned in their eulogies? It's such a common practice! So Ah Peng, do it without fear!"

I said, "All right, I'll do as you say."

Just then Party Secretary Shang walked in, looking travel-weary. The minute he came in the door, he said, "I'm glad to find you both here."

The Big Man asked if he had made his report to the county government yet.

Party Secretary Shang picked up the Big Man's cup and poured a mouthful of cold tea down his throat before saying he had, "Neither the county party secretary nor the county chief was in their office, so I reported it to Old Ji, the first deputy county chief."

The Big Man echoed, "You reported it to Ji Guodong. That's very good."

I exchanged a look with Party Secretary Shang. Ji Guodong had worked in the city agriculture department before taking up his post in the county government. He was designated a Senior Agronomist and was a technocrat in the county leadership. On a tour of the Tacheng Garden Farms some years back, he happened on Wei Shouyi cultivating out-of-season cucumbers inside a big greenhouse covered in film and asked a number of technical questions, to all of which Wei Shouyi gave articulate, convincing answers. On his return Ji Guodong said to Town Chief You Baida, "A great talent is right here under your nose! How come you haven't recognized it?"

You Baida answered that he had already planned on promoting Wei Shouyi to a leadership role. "With your nod, County Chief Ji, this will sail through more easily now."

Back in the county, Ji Guodong reported this matter to the county party secretary and the county chief. It happened that periodic elections for leadership positions were due for spring that year, and at the suggestion of the county government, the Tacheng town government immediately set to work and recruited, without going through too strenuous a campaign, Wei Shouyi into the town leadership team. It is fair to say that Ji Guodong, like the Big Man, saw Wei Shouyi as a promising future leader, and was one of the leading officials responsible for grooming Wei Shouyi for high office.

The Big Man asked, "What did County Chief Ji say?"

Party Secretary Shang said, "When I reported the matter to him, County Chief Ji had actually already been informed of Town Chief Wei's accident. He said members of the standing committee of the county party committee were also briefed. He said that Wei Shouyi was a worthy town chief who had made a unique contribution to both the town and the county and that the leadership mourned his death at so young an age and in such a tragic manner."

The Big Man said with a glance in my direction, "Ah Peng! Bear these words in mind!"

I nodded.

Party Secretary Shang said, "County Chief Ji also said that he would attend the memorial service for Town Chief Wei, and that he would find time one of these days to pay a visit of condolence to the grieving family and comfort them."

The Big Man said, "That's great! County Chief Ji and we are of one mind then. We must not delay our visit to Qin Dujuan. We don't want to appear less solicitous than County Chief Ji or passive and reactive in our work."

Party Secretary Shang said, "I agree. I told County Chief Ji that Wei's death had so far been kept from his family. He said that we couldn't expect to 'keep a fire wrapped up in a sheet of paper.' Truth will out. The family has to be told sooner or later. Sooner is better so that you keep the initiative. But he said we must be careful when we talk to the family to avoid shocking unduly them and further complicating things."

The Big Man agreed, "He's so right. County Chief Ji has thought of all the angles."

Party Secretary Shang said, "County Chief Ji also emphasized that in view of Wei Shouyi's sterling service, the town government could consider holding an elaborate memorial service for him and paying a generous sum in survivor benefits to the grieving family." He continued, "Don't underestimate the importance of the memorial service. A memorial service can influence public opinion. It is a show put up for the living. Nowadays young people make light of agriculture and stay away from first-line farm work. The rural exodus is an ominously growing trend. Bucking the trend, Wei Shouyi persevered in his farm work and achieved great results. By giving a cadre like him a grand funeral we can encourage more people to learn from him and follow in his footsteps."

The Big Man listened with a gleam in his eyes. He addressed me, "Ah Peng! Did you hear? These instructions of County Chief Ji's set the tone for how the town government should make the funeral arrangements."

I nodded.

Party Secretary Shang said, "Town Chief You! Why don't we strike while the iron is hot? Let's go visit Qin Dujuan now."

The Big Man readily agreed. He got up and called in the secretary, instructing him to request a sedan from the small-vehicle motor pool to take them to the town school.

I hastened to get my bag, and told them that earlier that morning the county traffic police brigade had turned over Town Chief Wei's personal effects to me that morning and suggesting they take them with them and give them to the family.

This announcement produced a simultaneous tremor in their eyes and the air seemed to gel all of a sudden.

I unzipped the bag in one quick stroke, and was going to imitate the policewoman at the traffic police brigade by turning it over and dumping its contents on the desk. On second thought I found it disrespectful, so holding my breath I gingerly took out from the bag the watch, the cell phone, the key ring and the wallet one item at a time and laid them on the Big Man's desk.

The Big Man and Party Secretary Shang quietly

followed the movements of my hand with their eyes and looked at the items in silence. As each item came out of the bag, they exchanged a glance; the Big Man was particularly affected: each time an item emerged from the bag, the muscles under his eyes would quiver. Finally the Big Man picked up that cell phone, his eyes reddening around the rims as he stroked it with his hand.

Party Secretary Shang picked up the bunch of keys with two fingers and closely examined that ivory chop seal, as if in reminiscence, and said softly, "His things are still here but the man is gone! The man is gone!"

The Big Man said, with a glance at Party Secretary Shang, "Do we just give these to Qin Dujuan?"

I said, "What other choice do we have?"

The Big Man said, "I have a feeling she might faint at the sight of them."

I asked him what else we could do.

The Big Man suggested, "I'm inclined to hold them for the moment and turn them over to the family at a suitable time."

I said anxiously, "Where are we going to keep them? Who will have temporary custody of them?"

The Big Man suggested he would take custody of them in the interim.

Party Secretary Shang abruptly blurted out, "Town Chief You! You are the chief executive of the town. We couldn't possibly trouble you to hold these items. My view is that, Town Chief Peng, we can leave these personal effects with you for temporary safekeeping."

I glanced at Party Secretary Shang but said nothing; deep down though I was not happy with the suggestion. I thought to myself: Party Secretary Shang! What do you mean by that? Why are you, the number one official in our town, micromanaging a trivial detail like this? What's wrong with the Big Man taking custody of Wei Shouyi's belongings?

But I did not have the courage to contradict Party Secretary Shang to his face. He was a seasoned leader with impressive credentials, including a stint as secretary to the county party secretary for many years, and a solid education. He was known not only for his extensive knowledge and experience, but his astuteness. Behind his back, many in the town government compound called him by the nickname "Old Whip," crediting him with infallible judgment and remarkable insight. The way he often dealt with things reminded one of a whip hitting hard and fast, drawing blood with every single lash. When he spoke, whether in the town government compound or outside it, we subordinates never dared say no.

Party Secretary Shang obviously saw through my mind and said, "Ah Peng, are you having any qualms about this? Are you superstitious? Afraid that holding these belongings of the deceased would bring bad luck? Hey, we are communists, and we believe in dialectical materialism! So what are you afraid of?"

I said sheepishly, "It's not that I am afraid of anything. These items are after all personal effects left behind by the dead, they are best held by the party organization ..."

Party Secretary Shang said, "I'm asking you to hold them in safekeeping for the party. Let me tell you: since this is official business and the party is doing it in the public interest, no ghost would knock on your door, if there were any."

Party Secretary Shang spoke in a loud and stern voice and, frankly, what he said made sense, so I resignedly put the items back into a big paper bag one by one, and holding the bag in my arms listlessly, followed them out of the Big Man's office, and watched them get into the car one after the other and disappear out of the compound gate.

As the car drove off, quiet returned to the compound and, with it, came that empty feeling again
and an impulse to sob.

All afternoon, although I sat physically in my
office, my mind wandered off, imagining how the
Big Man and Party Secretary Shang would meet and
speak with Qin Dujuan. I wondered how they would
break the news to that young woman and how they
would go about comforting her; and I wondered
how devastated Qin Dujuan would be when she was
given the bad news of her husband's death. As I sat by
the window looking at the desultory clouds drifting
across the sky, I vaguely heard, coming from the far
horizon, a woman's weeping, now loud, now weak,
now audible and now gone ...

4

I'd written a lot in my long career, but this was
the first time I was asked to write a eulogy. I asked
Little Li of the broadcast station to bring me several
months' worth of newspapers and I combed through
the obituary sections; before I finally put together a
rough draft, I had gone through two changes of tea

leaves in my cup. It read:

"Comrade Wei Shouyi, member of the Chinese Communist Party, Deputy Chief of the town of Tacheng, passed away in the night of April 21, xxxx, following an unfortunate traffic accident. He was 37.

"Comrade Wei Shouyi, born in the 1960s, had since a young age resolved to lift his impoverished home-town out of poverty. He studied hard and passed the test that led to his admission to the county agricultural vocational school. While attending that school, his academic excellence and exemplary behavior earned him the great honor of being recruited into the communist youth league. After graduation, he gave up the opportunity to work in the county government and returned to his home-town to participate in the creation of the Tacheng Garden Farms, soon becoming its first manager. Thanks to his trail-blazing work, the importance of Tacheng in the agricultural production of the county had grown from year to year and its agricultural output shown a remarkable increase. With a heavy emphasis on the role of science and technology, assiduous research and bold experimentation, he achieved breakthroughs in introducing foreign varieties of vegetables, catapulting Tacheng into the limelight as the foremost center of eco-friendly vegetable production in the entire county and the entire city and earning himself the highly esteemed title of 'Outstanding Agronomist.'

"In the four years as deputy town chief, Comrade Wei Shouyi resolutely implemented the platform agreed at the third Plenum of the 11th Communist Party of China Central Committee; he heeded the voice of the grassroots and worked diligently in the popular interest. His solid efforts bore fruit. By employing his intelligence and skills and mobilizing the town folk in science-based farming, he blazed a trail of scientific and technical innovation that brought prosperity to the farming community. His commitment to his work, his professional skills and tireless learning earned him the respect of cadres and the masses alike. His incorruptibility, rectitude and disinterest in personal enrichment won him acclaim in all walks of life in the town. In his sudden untimely death, the farmers have lost a good standard-bearer and we have lost a good town chief. The cadres and the masses of Tacheng Township deeply grieve his passing! "

As I wrote, I glanced at the now unoccupied desk opposite me and recalled all the days and nights

Wei Shouyi and I sat across from each other, and the thought came to me that even members of a family didn't get to spend as much time together, and I felt a sharp stab in my heart, and tears rolled down my cheeks, falling pitter-patter on the stationery paper.

Before I knew it a long time had gone by; I had done my deceased friend justice with an emotion-laden pen and my heart was full. I only realized the light had faded when the public address system started a broadcast outside.

I didn't feel hungry. After the tears, I felt light-headed and warm, like a mountain climber pausing at the top and finding his body refusing to immediately cool down because of the blood still racing through his veins. The functionaries of the town government had gone home for the day. Only the dim yellowish light of the gatehouse and the last golden afterglow in the west lighted the quieted compound. The public address system was playing "Wailing River," an *erhu* piece, occasionally punctuated by the chittering of birds in flight, sounds that spoke to my mood. The wind blew in through the half open south window; flaring my nostrils I sniffed at the air and detected a smoky smell from the burning of years-old hay in farmers' stoves. Bicycle bells sounded on the road outside the compound; the short bursts of ringing spoke of the rider's eagerness to go home.

I turned on the lamp and shifted in my chair to assume a more solemn posture and read out the eulogy to see if it sounded smooth. I'd only read a few lines when the phone rang.

Party Secretary Shang said on the phone, "Town Chief Peng, you're still in the office?"

I said, "The Big Man traded tasks with me. He wanted me to write Shouyi's eulogy."

Party Secretary Shang responded, "I want to speak to you about something. Is there anyone else in the office?"

I told him I was alone, "Go ahead."

Party Secretary Shang said in a lowered voice, "Do you understand why I wanted you to have custody of Wei Shouyi's belongings earlier in the day?"

I said that, in fact, I was confused, "If the Big Man wanted to hold them, why didn't you let him have custody of them? Why did you try to stop him?"

Party Secretary Shang said, "Ah Peng! You are naïve! Do you know why the Big Man wanted to keep those items in his safekeeping?"

I said, "I don't know. Why did he?"

Party Secretary Shang said, "He had his eyes on the bunch of keys."

I asked with a startled expression, "Keys? What keys?"

Party Secretary Shang said, "Wei Shouyi's keys."

I said, "I see. But even if he had the keys, what could he do with them?"

Party Secretary Shang answered, "He aimed to discover Wei Shouyi's secrets."

I was astounded and asked, "Why would he want to discover Wei Shouyi's secrets. What secrets did Wei Shouyi have that would be worth discovering?"

Party Secretary Shang said quietly, "I always suspected the Big Man and Wei Shouyi were in something together."

I asked, "In what areas?"

Party Secretary Shang spoke loudly, "What areas? All areas! Just wait and see, if you don't believe me. It is not unlikely that You Baida will still try to contact you and ask for the keys."

I said, "If he does come to me, should I or should I not give them to him?"

There was a sudden note of gravity in Party Secretary Shang's tone as he said, "Town Chief Peng! I'm saying this to you in all seriousness:

You must not give him the keys, absolutely not, you understand? If he asks you for them, tell him that Party Secretary Shang has spoken to you, and Town Chief Wei's belongings have been turned over to the party committee for safekeeping. Do you understand what I mean?"

I was somewhat nervous; I said I understood, but I did not fully get Party Secretary Shang's point, not really.

After I put down the phone, my head was abuzz with confusion. What was going on? What did he mean the Big Man and Wei Shouyi were in something together? What secrets were locked in those keys? And how did Party Secretary Shang find out about all that?

Suddenly I felt as if a black curtain had been pulled over my eyes and a shiver ran down my spine; a cold draft slithered along the floor and up the soles of my feet ...

Old Ding of the gatehouse chose this awkward moment when my hair was standing on end to poke his head around the window frame to ask in a whisper, "Town Chief Peng, I see you are still working. Would you like the kitchen to make you a bowl of noodle soup? You must be hungry."

Waving a hand, I said, "Run on! Don't let me take you away from your work. I'm still busy working on this."

Old Ding vanished like a ghost. I realized only then that a wind had risen and the millions of leaves on the two ancient camphor laurel trees in the yard, blown by the wind, made a loud rustling sound. The night got darker, and more clouds crowded the sky; against its faint light large masses of gray clouds jostled and drifted, as anxious and impatient as the humans down here.

A thought flashed through my mind: This guy, Party Secretary Shang, is known for his paranoid streak. He has a knack for making simple things complicated. Perhaps he was just being paranoid again.

I closed the window but still felt cold in my torso as well as in my limbs. I rose to my feet, rubbed my hands together, jumped, blew hot air into my hands, but none of that warmed me up. Then it hit me: As long as I am in this office, the cold will not be in my body but in my heart, and in my bones. I was tempted by the idea of burning some paper for the dead.

Burning paper in the office was probably unheard of in our compound. According to the folk custom of

the town of Tacheng, when someone dies, you need
to light a fire. You can either burn paper, or clothes,
or mosquito nets in the fire. It will supposedly drive
away evil spirits and bad luck; secondly it serves as
illumination to send the deceased on his way. The fire
should be situated next to a path most often used by
the deceased in his living days. It might not be a bad
idea to light a fire in this office, burning bright and
warm, to send Shouyi on his way, and to steady my
frazzled nerves.

But the fire would need to be hidden from the
others.

I fetched a pile of newspapers from the top of the
cabinets and found a batch of back-issue newsletters
in the corner of the room; then I brought in from
under the eaves of the corridor an old pottery
container, placed it in the middle of the office and
poured some water in it. As I got ready to light the
fire, I was bothered by the position of the container,
so I moved it a few feet closer to where Wei Shouyi
used to sit. This was the path most traveled by him
and it was littered with a few cigarette butts he threw
on the floor; at the foot of the file cabinets nearby
was a pair of "Liberation" shoes, still caked with
mud, from the days when he was sent down to the

countryside to be educated by the masses. I moved the shoes closer to the container and imagined I saw Wei Shouyi stepping up to the pot in those shoes. When I was all set to strike the match, I suddenly remembered that copy of the County Newspaper on Wei Shouyi's desk.

I'll use this as kindling, I thought. On its front page, the banner featured a photo of Wei Shouyi. It was his favorite photo: he stood in an aisle of the greenhouse, wearing a coat often donned by lab scientists, one hand on a foreign variety of cucumber about two spans long and the other hand holding a bunch of cherry tomatoes the color of carnelian, a cheerful but measured smile on his face.

With my eyes fixed on the photo of Wei Shouyi, I said in my heart, Shouyi, this is my own private farewell to you. To honor the memory of a departed friend, our forefathers often burned his poems; I'll burn a newspaper with a photo of you and a feature article full of praise for your achievements, right here where you used to work, hoping that it will be transformed into a wisp of smoke to follow you to the beyond. If there is that other world, then this article and this photo will keep you company and enable you to continue to feel proud and hold your head high.

I squat to strike a match and reverently kindled the newspaper, which was quickly charred and curled up in the flame. In the light yellow flames, the photo soon became charred and curled up too, and just before it turned to ashes, I thought I saw Wei Shouyi's smile sharpen in focus and at the same time I seemed to vaguely hear a peal of his laughter reverberating in the rafters of the room ...

My hair stood on end. I turned to look at the rafters, where there was a flickering play of light and shade caused by the leaping flames. When I listened more closely, I realized it was not human laughter but the crackling and popping of the flames.

The paper burned fast. I stood up, feeling light-headed. Scanning the walls and the ceiling, I was struck by the brightness and richness of the colors in the office lit up by flames. The brilliance reached the four corners of the room, illuminating the cobwebs and thick dust, giving off an eerie strangeness. I circled the burning pot twice, my lips moving, although I was unaware of what I was saying to the flame.

As the tongues of the fire rose and fell, the room alternately brightened and dimmed. Flakes of ash rose from the fire and spiraled up. The air quickly turned hot and dry. My cheeks started to burn and my limbs warmed up; my blood, as if thawed, began to flow again. In the expanding waves of heat, my breathing became labored. My eyes misted, from sorrow or from the stinging of the smoke—I wouldn't know.

Suddenly I heard my name called.

I shuddered and turned to look out the window. My eyes, dazzled and blurred from fixing on the flames for too long, couldn't make out at first who it was outside the window. I could, however, clearly sense a momentary pause in my heartbeat. I was acutely aware that in this town government compound, it was not a good thing to be caught burning paper in the office.

I heard two more knocks on the window and the call got louder. Then my vision cleared up; it was You Baida, Town Chief You, at the window.

I muttered, "Rats!" and got into a fluster: Should I immediately put out the fire? But then what was the use of dousing the flame since the Big Man had already seen it?

The Big Man came in and stared at the fire. His face was taut and he did not say a word.

I did not speak either. At a moment like this any explanation would sound lame.

The Big Man stood there, looking fixedly at the flame. After a moment he squat, picked up a few sheets of paper and slowly dropped them into the flame, watching them be devoured by it.

He rose to his feet and said to me, "It's good to light this fire. Good."

I breathed a little easier.

The Big Man continued to feed more paper into the fire and said as he did so, "Hey, Shouyi, what's the matter with you leaving us so soon? Without even a goodbye! You were so young, and a promising future was ahead of you. Now it falls to me, a silver-haired man, to see you to your grave. What were you thinking?"

As he spoke, tears rolled down his cheeks; in the glow of the flame, those tears appeared red, like blood.

Having burned all the paper near the pottery container, the Big Man stood up, clapping his hands to shake off the dirt. I opened the windows in two facing walls, and a refreshing whiff of night air with a nip in it blew in. As the roomful of smoke escaped through the north window, it gave way to a subtle fragrance of camphor laurel leaves that drifted in from the south window.

The Big Man came near my desk and his eyes fell on the eulogy I'd been composing. He pointed to it and said, "Ah Peng, you do write fast!"

I answered, "When you give me an assignment, I wouldn't think of taking my time carrying it out."

He scanned across the pages, his eyes pausing at certain paragraphs. I nervously awaited his judgment.

He read it three times; to me that felt like an eternity. Finally the Big Man put down the two sheets of paper, and spoke up, "Ah Peng, that was well-written! It covers most of the essential points of comrade Wei Shouyi's legacy. I only wish to bring up one thing."

I asked, "What is it you want to discuss?"

He said, "Can we say he died in the line of duty instead of in a traffic accident?"

I asked, "Well, did he die in the line of duty?"

He retorted, "How do you know he did not die in the line of duty? Didn't he often go out at night to represent the town government in business discussions?"

I said, "Or he might have driven while intoxicated after leaving a social gathering."

He said, "One discusses official business at social gatherings. Don't we cadres of the town government socialize and build a network of acquaintances precisely for the purpose of growing the town businesses? In the final analysis everything the town chiefs do is official."

What he said sounded reasonable to me. When I attended social activities, everybody I ran into appeared to have some official title. So I picked up my pen and changed "following an unfortunate traffic accident" to "in the line of duty."

The Big Man's face visibly softened. He said. "Much is at stake in determining whether it's death in the line of duty, death due to illness or death in an accident. Survivor benefits vary greatly, as well as future benefits the bereft family would enjoy. Ah Peng, Wei Shouyi's legacy and the future livelihood of Qin Dujuan depend to a large degree on this pen you are holding in your hand."

Town Chief You accompanied his words with gestures, looking very serious. I felt a burden on my mind and I said, "My role couldn't possibly be as pivotal as you make it out to be. The eulogy can still be changed as you like, but wouldn't it be up to the civil affairs department of the county to certify whether he died while on official duty? After all it's the county civil affairs department that disburses the survivor benefits."

The Big Man said, "That's for later; we will

not worry about it now. As long as we in the town government stick to our version of 'dying while on official business,' we can handle any objections or obstruction from them. If in the future the county government refuses to honor its obligation, then the town government will; if the county refuses to disburse the survivor benefits, I will! The county civil affairs department doesn't pay my salary, so what can it do to me?"

I nodded, picked up a broom to sweep up the ash strewn on the floor and scooped up a few handfuls of water and sprinkled them on the clay pot. Then I carried it outside.

When I returned to the office, the Big Man had already closed the windows. He crossed to Wei Shouyi's desk; after looking first at the photo calendar under the glass top, he plumped down on Wei Shouyi's chair and heaved a sigh.

I thought to myself: The Big Man is a tough guy. When he decides to do something he just forges ahead fearlessly. As old folks say, he is so full of yang energy that he is impervious to evil influence. As for me, I would be very inhibited and apprehensive; I wouldn't dare sit in Wei Shouyi's chair.

The Big Man motioned me to sit down, while

picking up a pack of cigarettes left on the desk by Wei Shouyi, getting one out and lighting it. He said, "Ah Peng, can I borrow that bunch of keys of Shouyi's?"

My nerves went taut as if bitten by a bug. When I gazed at the Big Man, what I saw was the face of Party Secretary Shang. I thought to myself: No wonder Party Secretary Shang is known in the compound as Old Whip. True to his nickname, he saw through the Big Man. He foresaw everything!

Tapping his fingers on Wei Shouyi's desk, the Big Man added, "A few days ago, I asked Shouyi to write a summary of the spring sowing operations in the entire town. He told me on the day of the accident the report was ready. I think he may have locked it in these drawers. I want to take a look at it as soon as possible; the county government has been rushing me."

As I listened to him, I thought: You Big Man are way outclassed by Party Secretary Shang! You can't even make up a convincing lie! Since when has a trivial thing like the summary report on spring sowing been personally handled by a deputy town chief? Isn't that what the town agricultural corporation is for? Even if we suppose, for argument's sake, the report is in Wei Shouyi's office, is it really necessary for you to make a special trip so late in the night to get it? What's the rush in a document as mundane as this?

Remembering the instructions of Party Secretary Shang, I replied calmly, "Town Chief, you have come too late."

The Big Man asked, with a twitch in his face, "Why? What happened?"

I said, "Party Secretary Shang came to me today. He knew I had qualms about keeping Wei Shouyi's belongings, so he took them off my hands."

The Big Man asked, "So you turned them over to him for safekeeping?"

I said, "What difference does it make who keeps them?"

With a rebuke, shaking his head and stamping a foot on the ground, the Big Man said, "That old whip! What an old whip!"

Then he shot a baleful glance at me.

Frankly I was a little frightened by the look in the Big Man's eyes. Party Secretary Shang is the top dog in the town and the Big Man is the executive chief of the town; both are my bosses and I couldn't afford to antagonize either of them. I had no idea why the Big Man was so worked up about this thing at this moment. What was so precious about those thingamajigs left behind by Wei Shouyi that he was so eager to get his hands on them? I had told him those items were now with Party Secretary Shang. Did that warrant his reaction? I didn't know what issues they had with each other.

I asked, "Do you want me to phone Party Secretary Shang now and ask him to bring Shouyi's keys?"

The Big Man answered gruffly, "Forget it!"

He sat grim-faced and uncommunicative for a while, then left. He slammed the door so hard when he made his exit that I nearly jumped out of my skin.

It was my turn to be vexed. I thought: This is between you two top leaders. It has nothing to do with me. You picked the wrong person to vent your temper on.

5

It was some time after the Big Man left that a sense of calm returned to me.

I opened my drawer and started putting things in order, getting ready to go home. My eyes were again drawn to that big paper bag holding Wei Shouyi's personal effects. I felt a sudden curiosity about the

Big Man's keen interest in that bunch of keys. Was there really some secret locked away in Wei Shouyi's drawers?

It was getting very late and the compound was now submerged in a deathly silence, except for the rustling of the leaves on the two ancient camphor laurels ruffled by occasional gusts of the night wind, and the mating calls from a couple of tree squirrels skittering under the corridor eaves, desperately seeking mates.

Somewhere a cuckoo sang—cuckoo, cuckoo, cuckoo. It's not often that one hears cuckoos sing at night. The singsong rose and fell in the rural night air, appearing now far away, now close by, the smooth, melodious, forlornly beautiful notes exercising a haunting, mysterious allure like the singing of a siren.

It was a night that invited wild, forbidden thoughts. I was seized by a sudden idea: should I open Wei Shouyi's drawers and find out what was in there?

I admit it was a despicable idea, but I couldn't help it. What was frightening is that once the idea was out of the bottle it swelled like a genie and took up all the space in my head. I walked around to Wei Shouyi's desk, where I stood as if in a trance, my eyes riveted by its top drawer.

I can imagine what a figure I cut at that moment. Surreptitious, wracked by anxiety and guilt and hesitation, I must have looked as nervous as a thief. I knew that what I was going to do would be a sacrilege to the dead; it would mean I was on the brink of moral bankruptcy.

The thought of moral bankruptcy gave me pause. I told myself I mustn't stoop to such a dishonorable act. After all, Wei Shouyi had been a good friend.

But, the secret jostling between Party Secretary Shang and the Big Man over the bag of Shouyi's belongings had whetted an intense longing in me to uncover the secret hidden in Wei Shouyi's drawer. The longing turned into an irresistible temptation ...

In short I wanted to take a look inside Wei Shouyi's drawer.

I returned to my desk and sat down; I reached into the paper bag and fumbled for the keys. The first thing that came into contact with my hand was that private chop on the key ring; the ivory seal felt smooth and pleasant to the touch. I lifted the chop, and the keys came out with a tinkling metallic sound.

With Wei Shouyi's private seal in my hand, I seemed to feel his body heat and see his smile. When I took it with me to sit in Wei Shouyi's chair and turn my eyes on the keyhole in the drawer, I was overwhelmed by a sense of guilt.

I said in my heart: Shouyi, sorry about this ...

Maybe it was panic, or unfamiliarity with the keys, but none of the keys I tried would unlock the top drawer; some of the keys didn't even fit into the keyhole. My panic grew worse. I saw Wei Shouyi in the photos under the glass top open his mouth in sinister laughter that echoed from different directions.

I tried the keys a second time. I was surprised myself that I had not the slightest intention to give up; on the contrary I was more determined than ever to open Wei Shouyi's drawer. I understood then why a thief in action would be so tenacious, so engrossed and so reckless; even when he knew there was no going back and a tragic ending awaited him, he would not stop ...

Then a terrible thing happened.

Someone knocked on the office door, and the key I just inserted into the keyhole somehow got stuck and refused to be extracted no matter how hard I tried to get it out!

My brain went into spasms. Unauthorized use of posthumous personal effects in official safekeeping ... to open the drawer of someone who had died recently ... What are you doing?

The ability to think escaped from me, and my brain went blank.

Without leaving the chair, I turned toward the door and asked, "Who is it?"

There was no reply. After an interval of several seconds, I heard another three light knocks.

The knocking sounded unfamiliar to me. In our compound the staff banged on doors and did not knock discreetly like this.

Was it an auditory illusion? Or was it Wei Shouyi returning from the beyond to visit retribution on me for my perfidious act?

A cold sweat broke out on my back. I desperately pulled on the key but couldn't free it.

This must be poetic justice, I thought to myself. The door had to be answered. In despair, I sighed and, forcing myself to be calm, rose to open the door.

I was flabbergasted by what I saw—

Wei Shouyi's wife, Qin Dujuan, stood at the door, looking at me.

Qin Dujuan and I had been co-workers for many years. Before becoming deputy town chief, I taught high school math in the town school; in the fourth year of my tenure Qin Dujuan was assigned, upon graduation from the provincial normal college, to our town school, also as a math teacher. The day she reported for duty, the principal asked me to bring her with me to my classes to familiarize her with classroom processes, to break her in, as it were.

She had clean, regular features, was a soft speaker and had a demure demeanor. At our first meeting, the principal had us—the tutor and the tutee—shake hands. Her hand felt, in my grip, slender-boned and cool to the touch; when her eyes met mine, I had a premonition that something would happen between us.

And something did happen. During that period I took her under my wing and we grew to like each other. At our age we knew how to read each other's eyes; soon we got closer still.

The principal, ever solicitous for my well-being, asked me privately how it was going and whether I found the tutelage rewarding. He said he was motivated by two considerations, "Firstly you are a distinguished teacher and the school needs someone to carry on your good work; secondly, you are not that young anymore. Are you going to remain single for the rest of your life? In my observation, Teacher Qin is a quiet and thoughtful lady and she is so pleasant to be with. You two would be a perfect match."

I said to the principal, "How can you think of a thing like that? If I did such a thing with a teacher I'm meant to be counseling, it'd raise a storm of criticism."

The principal said with a smile, "What's there to criticize? Teacher-student romances are forbidden in our school, but there's nothing against love between teacher and teacher-trainee. I encourage you, Teacher Peng, to seize the opportunity while it's there. You can't find many pretty and smart ladies like Teacher Qin in our town. If someone else gets to her while you procrastinate, you'll hate yourself for it!"

Unfortunately, his words were prophetic.

That winter, the town government had its eyes on me as candidate for Deputy Town Chief for Education and Culture. Soon I was transferred from the town school to the training program for party cadres sponsored by the county party committee for six months of learning and training. In those hectic few months I was given a long reading list, had to take and pass tests, and trot off to different neighboring counties and travel farther afield to study and learn from others' experiences and best practices; I was on the road so much my right foot and left foot were tripping each other. I had thought the stint at the party cadre school would be an opportunity to enjoy some rest and recuperation and recoup my strength for a romantic assault on Qin Dujuan upon my return. But I hadn't counted on all the grueling eye-straining reading I had to do and the considerable weight loss I would experience. And I could not have predicted what lay ahead. When I completed the six-month program and returned to the town school I learned to my dismay that Qin Dujuan had in the meantime taken up with Wei Shouyi, the manager of the Garden Farms next to the school. Wei Shouyi had even taken her to meet his parents at their home on a vacation day. It was unclear whether they had spent the night there.

I nearly fainted when they broke the news to me. I couldn't get over the fact that she did it. Wasn't she a quiet and thoughtful young lady with "nice" written all over her lovely face? It's not as if she and I had not exchanged amorous glances and meaningful smiles at each other all that time, with mutual affection unspoken but understood; how was it that in the short span of a few months, she had turned her back on me and run to another man without even a goodbye?

That night my anger was so great I felt a constriction in my chest and my liver hurt; I tossed and turned all night in bed. It was not until I went out at first light the next day, climbed to the roof of the school building to take some fresh air and serendipitously witnessed a sunrise from beginning to end that I succeeded in sorting out my emotions a little bit. I berated myself on the rooftop: You are pathetic! Isn't there an ounce of manliness in you? There's no point in demanding an account from a gentle, fragile woman. What right do you have to grudge her seeing another man? What's so special between her and you? Has she vowed eternal love to you? Or slept with you? No and no. Then what obligation did she have toward you? Why should she have waited for your return?

Easy to say, but my heart was bleeding. Whenever I spotted her from afar anywhere on the campus, I'd have an urge to stamp my foot on the ground.

When the good principal, ever solicitous of his staff's welfare, found out about it, he called in Qin Dujuan for a talk and asked her what was going on.

The first thing Qin Dujuan had said to the principal was, "I still hold a soft spot in my heart for Teacher Peng."

The principal asked, "If that was the case, why

did you start seeing someone else?"

She said. "When Teacher Peng left for the county party cadre training program, I missed him very much. I wrote him a letter the very next day; it was not about anything in particular, just to ask him how he was, and tell him to take care of himself and keep in touch. I waited eagerly for a reply, but after a fortnight I was still waiting and nothing came from him. I got worried and wrote two more letters, which also went unanswered. I was disillusioned, and chided myself for being infatuated with someone who did not return my affection and for misinterpreting kindness as romantic interest. I realized that since Teacher Peng was attending the party school and being groomed for higher office, he had a promising career in government. He had no conceivable reason to want a romantic relationship with an insignificant teacher like me. As I grappled with these thoughts, Wei Shouyi, the manager of the Garden Farms, started bringing me movie tickets, chatting and playing ping-pong with me and taking me window-shopping in the streets of the newly developed communities. One thing led to another and before long we were dating regularly."

The principal faithfully relayed all this to me. Stamping my foot, I cried out, "Letters my foot! I never received any letters from her!"

The principal asked. "You really didn't receive any letter from her?"

I said, "Really! Not one letter! Heaven be my witness! If I lied, I'd be struck dead by lightning!"

With an "ah!" the principal lapsed into silence.

I was mystified by the three letters allegedly addressed to me.

Their courtship progressed by leaps and bounds. Shortly after Shouyi and I took up our new duty in the town government, they got their marriage certificate at the civil affairs department. A few days before the nuptial banquet, they sent me a formal invitation.

It was, I remember, a night before the May 1st Labor Day. I was struck dumb as I held the invitation in my hand. I reasoned with myself as best I could: Be a man! Know when to let go! I had to attend the wedding party, not only because I was Qin Dujuan's trainer but also because Wei Shouyi and I were colleagues in the town government. If I didn't go, my reputation would suffer and people would think me petty.

I attended the wedding banquet and brought a gift of 2,800 yuan, an auspicious figure, because the Chinese pronunciation of 28 is close to "two, lucky." Seeing the beautiful bride and the handsome bridegroom, and detecting in the depth of Qin Dujuan's eyes an elusive look of uncertain meaning, I felt a stab in my heart. I feigned indifference and nonchalance, gulping down shot after shot of hard liquor, refusing none, and even going out on the offensive with cup in hand looking for anyone who would drink with me. Before the party was over, I had succeeded in making a fool of myself, staggering to the floor and vomiting uncontrollably.

It was the principal who took me home. When he helped me into my apartment, he tried to comfort me, "Ah Peng! Don't be so pig-headed. So Qin Dujuan married someone else; you can always find another woman. As they say, there are plenty more fish in the sea."

Who would have thought that barely two years after Qin Dujuan and Wei Shouyi got hitched, he would lose his life in a terrible accident. We can never tell what fate has in store for us.

6

Qin Dujuan stood before me.

I rested my eyes on her face for only a few seconds

before quickly looking away. The face I saw still had its delicate features, but her eyes were now surrounded by dark circles, which were a clear indication of the deep sorrow she was suffering.

I let her into the office. My first thought was to have her sit in a chair by my desk for fear that she might see that key stuck into her husband's drawer. I swallowed before saying in a lowered voice, "Have a seat."

She didn't sit down but stayed stiffly on her feet.

I said, "I finished writing Shouyi's eulogy. Would you care to have a look?"

I handed the sheets of paper to her. She didn't take long to finish reading it and when she handed the sheets back to me, she said, "Don't you think you overpraised him?"

I was startled, "What do you mean?"

She said, "He was not as good as you made him out to be."

I questioned, "Really?"

She repeated, "Really, he was not as good as you made him out to be."

She was quite serious when she said it. I got nervous and hastened to add, "I wrote this eulogy in the way suggested by Party Secretary Shang and the

Big Man. The Big Man already gave his approval after reading it."

A wry smile crossed Qin Dujuan's face as she said. "Write what you want. No matter how good you make him look, it's meaningless now."

I gaped at her, not knowing what to reply.

After a while, she asked suddenly, "You have Shouyi's keys, don't you?"

Exactly the question I didn't want to answer! I was so guilt-ridden I could hardly breathe. I said, "Yes."

She said, "Let me have them."

She spoke in a soft voice but it had a hard edge that allowed no refusal. I flinched, my eyes surreptitiously glancing at Shouyi's drawer.

Trying to stall for time I said, "The traffic police turned over some of Shouyi's stuff to me; there may be a few other things that I need to sort through. I'll turn everything over to you after I'm done."

She said, "I want the keys now, the rest can wait."

I started. Why is she so fixated on the keys also? Is she doing this at the behest of the Big Man? Could the situation really be as intrigue-ridden and tangled as this?

With these thoughts in my mind, I stole a glance

at her. I was nonetheless persuaded that I had no plausible reason to spurn her request. She was after all the widow of Wei Shouyi.

I took another furtive look at Wei Shouyi's drawer. Weighing the matter in my mind, I said, "All right, you'll have the keys. But can you step out of the room for a moment?"

With a dubious look at me, she left the room and pulled the door shut.

I dashed to Wei Shouyi's desk and pulled at the key. Mirabile dictu! The key slipped out with only a little coaxing! I was hugely relieved.

I opened the door to readmit Qin Dujuan and handed the keys to her.

She glanced at the ivory seal on the key ring and as she stroked it with her hand her eyes instantly reddened around the rims.

The sight saddened me, but I didn't know what to say to console her.

Putting the keys in her pocket, she said, "I'm leaving now."

"Don't you want to open Shouyi's drawer to take a look?" I asked.

She lifted her head and her eyes, misted up by tears, rested briefly on my face. Then she said, "That can wait."

I couldn't help asking, "Then why did you ask for the keys?"

She answered, "Because I lost my keys. I was distraught. After Party Secretary Shang and Town Chief You had a talk with me, I lost my head, and then I looked everywhere and couldn't find my house keys, which had always been in my bag."

With that, she turned and left. In the obscurity of night, she still cut a fascinating figure viewed from behind, and her footsteps still tapped out an ear-catching rhythm.

I endured a wakeful night. The images of Wei Shouyi and Qin Dujuan took turns floating before my eyes. Wei Shouyi's laughter and Qin Dujuan's weeping rang in my ears. The gray Passat and that body of ice-cold river water bobbed above and below the surface of my consciousness ...

I got up early the next morning still drowsy and was ready to go out to the town center for a cup of strong tea and a bite of dried tofu in sauce. But the moment I opened the door, I found the daylight blocked by a wall in the form of Qiu Sanbao.

Sanbao said in a lowered tone, "Anybody inside?"

The nervousness in his face made me anxious. I motioned him to a chair and asked him what brought him there this early in the morning.

Sanbao said, "Take back these two cartons of cigarettes first! Then we'll talk."

I immediately saw that they were the same two cartons of "Zhonghua" cigarettes I'd placed on the back seat of the police car he was driving and I was not pleased. I said. "Hey, Sanbao, so you think you are somebody now because of that uniform you're wearing. I may not be a big shot but at least I'm chief of the People's Government of a town. Are you worried that I was trying to bribe you with two cartons of cigarettes?"

Sanbao said, "Let's not go there. Take back those cartons; then we'll talk."

I grabbed the cartons and threw them from a distance on the desk, accidentally knocking a blue-and-white porcelain cup to the floor, shattering it and spilling the tea and tea leaves. I left the mess on the floor.

Sanbao said, "I see that Town Chief Peng has taken offense."

I gave him a withering look and said ungraciously, "Since you don't consider me a friend, do whatever you have to do by the book. Out with it then! Let's talk official to official."

Shaking his head, Sanbao lit a cigarette and said, "This is urgent, so I'm not going to argue with you. For your information, something turned up in the investigation into Wei Shouyi's accident. Why else would I have come to you this early in the morning?!"

I said, "Don't keep me guessing, just tell me."

He paused and answered, "We got the Passat out of the river last night. And guess what? We found one brown high heeled shoe on the back seat."

I was taken aback, "No kidding?"

Sanbao continued, "That's not all. There was also a black bra."

I couldn't stay seated anymore. I got up and walked around the room a few times and looked out the window for a long moment before I could breathe evenly again. I asked, "What would be the implications, I mean, according to the the police's assessment?"

Sanbao said, "It's hard to say. I told you then that it was strictly a one-car traffic accident that involved no one but the deceased. That no longer seems to be the case given this latest discovery."

"How so?" I asked him.

"With the discovery of these female articles, it's harder to close the case. After the car was hoisted out of the water, we found that one rear door was left open, which means when Wei Shouyi drove the car into the river, there was someone else in the car, a woman, who escaped by opening a rear door before the car sank," he explained.

I caught my breath and my temples started throbbing.

Sanbao went on, "Since there was a passenger in the car, we can no longer come to a clean, simple conclusion about the nature of the accident at this moment. And we can't be sure it was strictly a traffic accident."

"You're suggesting that this calls for a criminal investigation?"

Sanbao answered, "We can't rule out the possibility. Just imagine. A man and a woman in a car that plunged into the river! How much more complicated can it get? We already reported the matter to the county police and were told by the police chief that he would offer the services of their forensic team to help with the investigation of the case."

I took a deep breath and exhaled slowly, directing my breath out the window. The small town was awakening in the first light and the ancient streets started to fill with pedestrians and the noise and clamor of a bustling town—vegetable farmers hawking their produce, town folk haggling, porters yelling at people to get out of their way, bells on carts collecting night soil ringing, motorcycles' motors revving and the metal turner of a street vendor making pancakes clattering. People were too busy to care about what was going on in this room.

I turned from the window and went to pick up the two cartons of Zhonghua cigarettes. I said to Sanbao, "I know where you are coming from: you have no say in the determination of the nature of this accident. Am I right?"

"But what does that have to do with you?" I continued, "And why does that have anything to do with these cigarettes? If you don't take these two cartons, you are no damn friend of mine!" I added.

Qiu Sanbao declined a few more times before accepting the cartons and leaving my apartment.

I was left limp and weak as if my body had been stripped of its tendons and ligaments; my brain was addled and no longer could tell what time it was and I had no sense of what to do. I threw myself like a bundle of dried twigs onto my bed.

Now a pair of woman's high heels and a bra had been found in Wei Shouyi's car. What could it mean? Was Wei Shouyi up to some hanky-panky with a woman in the car before the crash?

Several scenarios ran through my mind:

Wei Shouyi was driving late at night on the County Road, with a woman in the back seat. As the car sped in the night, they got reckless and started groping each other. In the darkness of night, the car, carrying the wanton laughter of the two, their ecstasy and their terror at the last moment, had shot off the road into the river ...

Or alternatively: Could the woman have caused Wei Shouyi's death? She tied a rope or an electric cord around Wei Shouyi's neck and tightened it to choke the air out of him ... As Wei Shouyi struggled, he lost control of the steering wheel and drove the car across the sandbank and into the river ...

But why would this woman want to kill Wei Shouyi? Were they having an illicit affair or was there a darker secret? Did Wei Shouyi's body exhibit any signs of having been deliberately harmed?

Then there was a third possibility: Wei Shouyi, intent on ending the woman's life, deliberately crashed his car into the river. The only thing he hadn't reckoned with was that instead of doing in the woman he got himself killed ...

I even came up with a fourth and a fifth scenario: The possibility that more than two people were in the car. Was Wei Shouyi the victim of a robbery? Or could he have run into a prostitute and brought her into the car to have sex with her and left his soul behind in the icy river after an orgasmic explosion of pleasure?

7

I drifted off to sleep. When I opened my eyes again, the sun had already lit up a corner of the window. My eyes were gummed up, my skin was rough and wrinkled, my lower lip was cracked, and I could smell my own bad breath and my saliva was sticky. I realized I was suffering from excessive internal heat because I'd been obsessed with all those grotesque and far-fetched thoughts.

Giving up hope of going back to sleep I sat up and mulled over Qiu Sanbao's words, and recalled the scene by the river and ended up chiding myself. You are making this sound like *Murder on the Nile*! You, Mr. Peng, couldn't possibly aspire to be a detective, could you? Wei Shouyi was deputy chief of a little town and he merely had a car accident in the darkness of night. It was as simple as that.

Thus berating myself I descended the stairs to go to a teahouse. On the way I reflected on the eulogy I'd written. It said Wei Shouyi died while on official duty. What was I to do with that now? That conclusion no longer appeared tenable given the discovery of one woman's shoe and a bra in his car. Could one defend the position that he died while on official duty when the man sank to the bottom of the river, bringing down with him intimate female articles? Should I report this matter to Party Secretary Shang and the Big Man?

I quickly dismissed the idea, thinking that given the complexity of the investigation, the detail about the female articles in the car could be left aside for the moment. It would not be too late to report to them when Qiu Sanbao came out with something more definite and I wouldn't be accused of not keeping my cool by the Big Man and Party Secretary Shang. These days I would lay low, away from the town government compound and avoid seeing any colleague or members of the town leadership. After all it was they who tasked me with taking care of the aftermath of the accident involving Wei Shouyi with the county government, ironing out all problems and addressing all issues before coming back to town.

You before I arrived at the teahouse, I could already smell the smoke and steam billowing from its stove and the aroma of marinated eggs and tofu in tea sauce. I was famished. I quickened my pace and took out my wallet to get some change ready. Just when I stepped onto the town bridge, I was surprised by the sight of Qin Dujuan coming toward me.

Qin Dujuan wore a black crepe band around her left arm, which I found jarring. Her face seemed to have become gaunt overnight and her cheekbones stood out, the color had left her lips and her eyes had sunk, with black circles around them. She looked as if she had just emerged from a major illness.

She approached me and said, "I've been looking for you."

I asked, "What's up?"

She answered, "I'd like you to accompany me to the town government office to open the drawers of Wei Shouyi's desk."

I was hesitant; I'd decided to stay away from the office for now.

She glanced at me and explained, "The funeral

is only a few days away. There will be relatives and friends visiting and the local custom of hosting a tofu banquet has to be observed. I'm going to need some cash and he had all the bank account books, so I need to find them and also to take the opportunity to get his stuff together."

After considering it, I said, "I have to go to the county government office in the morning, so I won't be able to go with you. There should be a key to the office on Shouyi's key ring. You can let yourself in and take all the time you need to sort through his stuff."

Qin Dujuan said, "I've given some thought to this matter, I still think it would be better if you'd come with me. It was Wei Shouyi's office and it is also your office, so it wouldn't be prudent for me to go in by myself."

A wistfulness was added to the sadness in her eyes. My heart sank. I thought to myself, "Yes, why all the excuses? You and Wei Shouyi shared the same office for so long, and now you can't even satisfy a little request like this from his wife. It's unconscionable!"

I said, "All right," and went quickly into the teahouse to get a few pieces of tofu and two marinated eggs, trotted out my bicycle and pedaled toward the town government compound with Qin Dujuan on the back rack.

No wall is without cracks. By now news of Wei Shouyi's accident had leaked out and every cadre of the town bureaucracy had learned of it. When they saw me and Qin Dujuan enter the compound on a bicycle, they trained their sights on us immediately. There was a look of surprise and sympathy on their faces when they saw the black crepe on Qin Dujuan's arm, but not one of them stepped forward to greet us.

I opened the office door and stood aside to let her in. The smoky smell of burning paper from the other night still lingered and rushed at us the moment the door was opened. I opened the south and the north windows and said to Qin Dujuan: Take your time. If you need me, just holler. I will be in the broadcast station upstairs.

I freely admit that I got faint-hearted. I did not have the heart to watch Qin Dujuan open her late husband's drawer and how she would cope with Wei Shouyi's sudden departure, leaving everything behind. Frankly, ever since Qiu Sanbao told me that morning about the woman's shoe and bra found in Wei Shouyi's car, my suspicion had deepened about the contents locked away in Wei Shouyi's drawer. I remembered that he received frequent calls from a woman and he would hem and haw and speak in an oblique way, clearly embarrassed by my presence. Soon I learned to tactfully exit the office whenever such calls came in so that he could speak freely. I had long suspected that Wei Shouyi had a weakness for amorous adventure and that he had been unfaithful to Qin Dujuan.

I saw Qin Dujuan slowly get the bunch of keys out of her bag. I was terrified by the thought that when she opened Wei Shouyi's drawer, she would find incriminating evidence of infidelity, such as photos, love letters, tokens of love, and diaries. They would have nothing to do with me but I dreaded them all the same.

While he'd admittedly not gone out in a blaze of glory in the line of duty, Shouyi had met with a tragic end. Therefore I'd come to the view that he should be allowed a peaceful and clean exit, without leaving any taint of stigma or scandal to the living, especially Qin Dujuan, a woman and a teacher, who could least afford it.

Wei Shouyi and Qin Dujuan were much envied as a couple in the town government compound. They were considered a happy couple. They publicly stated after their wedding that they would not consider having a child in the first three years of their marriage. That was already very avant-garde in the town. What it meant was that without a child to take care of, the two could spend their income on themselves only and the couple lived every day as if they were still on their honeymoon; the nightly conjugal bliss in the newlyweds' bedroom simply tempted one's imagination and had the whole town envious. In the early days of their marriage, whenever Shouyi left a meeting with his team at the town government that ended later than usual, he would find Qin Dujuan waiting at the entrance of the compound for him, rain or shine, without fail. When it rained they preferred to huddle tightly together, almost fusing into one, under one umbrella. And when Qin Dujuan did not come home at the usual time because she had to make up a missed lesson, Shouyi would go to her school and wait at the entrance for her; sometimes he would bring snacks, like peanuts, to temporarily assuage her hunger. The other teachers at the town school were green with envy at these acts of spousal devotion. But in the past year such instances had dwindled. Town folk explained it away by saying that they must have realized they were no longer newlyweds and worried that if they continued this public display of affection, they'd only earn public ridicule. I alone was on to Shouyi's shenanigans with this woman who kept calling him on the phone and guessed something was awry; but when it came to specifics, I was as ignorant as the next person. One thing was certain though: Qin Dujuan was in the dark about all these goings-on in the office.

It's just as well that she be in the dark, I thought. The dead carry many secrets with them into their graves and it's best that others, including those closest to them, are kept in the dark about them. For this reason I truly did not wish for Qin Dujuan to find any indication of Wei Shouyi's infidelity or see anything that might traumatize her. Shouyi was after all an excellent town leader who had brought real progress and benefits to the town folk. Besides, he was still lying quietly in the county traffic police's ice cold morgue and had not yet completely evaporated from this world ...

When Qin Dujuan saw me pick up my tea cup and get ready to leave the room, she anxiously pleaded with me. "Teacher Peng, don't go."

I said, "Why?"

Qin Dujuan said, "To be frank ... I'm a little frightened. Can you please stay around and watch?"

I said, "These are Shouyi's private and personal things. It would not be ... convenient to have me at your side when you sort through it."

Qin Dujuan said, "It's all right. You can just sit there. Besides, there must be some official documents and stuff in his drawer. I'd feel more comfortable to have you watch over what I'll be doing."

I thought about it and said. "All right. I picked up a newspaper and sat down by the window to read it."

While ostensibly reading the paper, I was agitated and distracted. I pricked up my ears to follow the movements of her hands and feet and cast nervous glances out of the corner of my eyes to find out which drawer she had worked up to.

It appeared Qin Dujuan was as unfamiliar with Wei Shouyi's drawers as I was. She tried many different keys before she finally opened the first drawer. She went through the side drawers on the right very quickly, closing them after riffling through the contents cursorily. But when she opened the largest drawer in the middle, I saw her hand flinch as if she'd touched a live wire and she reflexively closed the drawer, but only half way.

She froze for a good moment, during which

my breath was suspended as was hers. I wondered if she'd seen something that broke her heart, or found a photo of another woman posing with Shouyi.

A full half minute went by before Qin Dujuan said slowly, "Teacher Peng, can you come over here for a moment?"

I put down my paper and crossed the room to Shouyi's desk. As Qin Dujuan slowly pulled the drawer out, she raised her eyes to my face.

Neat bundles of hundred-yuan notes taking up nearly half of the drawer's space leapt at my eyes. I was dumbfounded: how did Wei Shouyi get his hands on so much cash?

Qin Dujuan said, "He never let on to me that he had stashed away so much cash."

Her eyes reddened around the rims. I counted the half-drawerful of notes: There were 42 stacks of them, tightly tied with paper strips stamped with the bank teller's personal chop. Apparently those stacks of cash had not been touched since being withdrawn from the bank. The style and pattern of the stamped name bore some resemblance to that of Shouyi's ivory seal.

Qin Dujuan asked me, "How much was in there?"

I said, "420 thousand."

Qin Dujuan remembered, "He was always complaining that he was strapped for cash!"

She spoke in a low, melancholy voice laden with deep resentment and pain. After a while she suddenly asked me, "How did a town chief get hold of so much cash?"

I was stumped for an answer. It mystified me too.

Qin Dujuan asked, "Do you have money stashed away?"

I said with a wry laugh, "I am single, so I have no need to hide my money from anybody."

There was a quiver in Qin Dujuan's eyes when she whispered, "I'm sorry."

I said, "That's all right." But even before Hu Lanping and I were divorced, I did not keep any money on the side for myself. I used to have a few thousand yuan, tops, that I could draw on in case some friend or relative needed to be bailed out of a temporary financial bind.

After a while, Qin Dujuan continued, her eyes resting on the cash. "It appears to me ... this doesn't strike me as his private piggybank."

I said, "Who knows. Shouyi had a wide network of contacts and acquaintances and went into business for himself. It is not impossible that this is money he had laid away from the business deals."

Qin Dujuan fell silent. She was seated and I was on my feet. Looking down from above her I saw first a black crepe flower pinned in her hair, then I saw her whole body was shaking and the trembling was even more pronounced in her hands.

The air in the office seemed to have coagulated. Snatches of music drifted in from the public address speakers erected in the fields; it was that plaintive violin concerto entitled *Butterfly Lovers*. Occasionally one could hear a bicycle rushing across the yard and Old Ding of the gatehouse calling out to someone in the compound to take a phone call. The swarms of birds that used to leap from branch to branch among the ancient camphor laurels and disturb the peace with their chittering had deserted their normal haunt, restoring an unusual quiet to the compound. My wonder at this rare quiet was interrupted by the singing of a cuckoo a great distance away—cuckoo, cuckoo, cuckoo, cuckoo—soft, but clear and crisp, reminiscent of fields of reeds and plantings in the morning sun.

I glanced at the woman before me and suddenly remembered her name—Dujuan.

Dujuan is another name for the cuckoo—I

learned that from Teacher Xu many years ago. Probably Qin Dujuan herself didn't realize this, but it had been often on my mind. People are ambivalent about the cuckoo, which is considered by some to be a bird that brings good luck and by others to be one of ill omen. Teacher Xu had adamantly refused to eat a cuckoo, probably for good reason. Miao Zhigao killed two cuckoos with a catapult and at a later stage of his life committed a capital offense. Wasn't that proof of the bird's ability to bring bad luck? Wei Shouyi took Dujuan from me, and now he met a tragic end. Further proof of the cuckoo's evil influence? If Wei Shouyi hadn't come between us years ago and Qin Dujuan and I had gotten together, what turn would my life have taken? And how would our married life have fared?

I did not wish to compare myself with Miao Zhigao and Wei Shouyi. I believed that if I had married Qin Dujuan, we would have lived a peaceful life and our marriage would have been strong, because we were meant for each other and our union would not have been driven by any ulterior motives ...

All of a sudden Qin Dujuan called out, "Teacher Peng."

I started, "What's the matter?"

Qin Dujuan lifted her head to look at me with entreating eyes, "I need your advice. What should I do with this money?"

The look in her eyes pained me. I thought: Fate has been unfair to this suffering woman. Her marriage to a man like Wei Shouyi had not brought her much in the way of happiness and in the long days ahead she will be no stranger to more suffering. I said with mock levity, "If you ask me, the answer is simple! Just take home everything you find in Shouyi's drawers; if you don't, the town government will not know what to do with them."

Qin Dujuan said, "This is a lot of money. How can I take it home just like that? I wouldn't have peace of mind if I did ..."

I wondered, "Why wouldn't you have peace of mind? It's your husband's money, the wife can use it anyway she chooses. That's what Hu Lanping did with my money; she never bothered to ask where it came from. She just spent it."

Qin Dujuan said, "Your situation was different."

I answered, "Different or not, you can't go wrong spending Wei Shouyi's money. Since the money is here in Wei Shouyi's drawer, it is his money. Nothing on it says it's public funds. If the town government's money were in Wei Shouyi's drawer, you would have heard from the Big Man and Party Secretary Shang."

After a pause, Qin Dujuan said, "All right then, I'll take this cash home for now. If it is determined to be public funds, I will return it. What do you think?"

I said, "Good, you do that!"

Qin Dujuan wrapped the stacks of cash in a newspaper and put them into a plastic bag. She then tied the top of the bag securely and placed it on the desk near the wall.

It was obvious that once she found the cash, Qin Dujuan became distracted and more relaxed; the rest of her rummaging was cursory, until she came to the very back of the drawer near the left corner. Again she was startled, as if she had just touched a snake.

I followed the direction of her gaze and saw three letters in envelopes that had yellowed with time.

Qin Dujuan's face turned instantly ashen. She grabbed the three letters, taking each of them out of its envelope, her eyes rigid and harsh, shooting off cold sparks.

She said, "Teacher Peng, look!"

I couldn't believe my eyes—

That envelope bore the address of the party school of the county party committee, my name, and the words "for his personal attention!"

It was in Qin Dujuan's hand!

Gray, heart-breaking memories rolled in like high tide, making me gasp for air and sending me reeling.

I was in a daze as I stared at the three letters.

All three letters had been torn open, just like the reopened wound in my heart. The tear was irregular, an indication of the roughness with which the envelope had been ripped open. This was my first sight of my name written in Qin Dujuan's hand. She wrote a fine, regular hand; the penmanship appeared unfamiliar and yet possessed of a power to call one back from a great distance. But faced with this call to come home, what could I say?

Tears began to stream down Qin Dujuan's cheeks. With her hand pressing on the envelopes, she said amid sobs, "Who would have thought, who would have thought ..."

Looking at the black crepe flower in her hair, I heaved a long sigh. In hindsight, it was not such an unthinkable act. The town school and the Garden Farms were situated on opposite sides of the County Road, and the school's newspapers and mail were received care of the gatehouse/mailroom of the

Garden Farms. Because of the great distance to the town center the teachers would regularly leave their outgoing letters with the gatekeeper of the Garden Farms, so that the town mailman could pick them up on his mail route. Qin Dujuan must have done this with the letters addressed to me. How could she have known that even before they left the Garden Farms gatehouse, those letters had been intercepted and read—not by me, but by the man who was to become her husband?

Qin Dujuan put the three letters in my hand, her teary eyes looking at me, as if the letters vindicated her, and at the same time she seemed to want to say something. She muttered haltingly, "Teacher Peng ..."

The wrenching pain of years ago revisited me. I thought to myself: This is fate! This is fate! If these three letters had gone out as intended and arrived at my desk in the party school of the county party committee, my life would have been very different. I certainly would not have allowed myself to be introduced to Hu Lanping, and naturally would not have committed the folly of becoming married to and then divorced from her. I would surely have continued my courtship of Qin Dujuan and perhaps we would have got married and would likely have had children, who would be as beautiful as she was ...

After she had gone through all the drawers, I had Qin Dujuan take off all the house keys from Wei Shouyi's key ring and return the rest to me. I put the bunch of keys and the rest of Wei Shouyi's belongings back into a paper bag. I had no desire to let anybody find out what Qin Dujuan and I had privately done together.

I locked the paper bag away in my drawer and said to Qin Dujuan, "If anybody from the town government asks you, don't tell him you've seen the inside of Wei Shouyi's drawers."

Qin Dujuan asked, "Why?"

I answered, "No reason."

She said, "Does it have anything to do with the cash?"

I said, "It's not as complicated as you imagine. Most things in life are not that complicated."

She said, "But I'm concerned about where the money may come from."

I said, "Dubious provenance or not, it has nothing to do with you. Forgive me for sounding blunt and rude, but you won't ever come into this much money again. Before you hear from me again, don't say a thing to anybody about this, understand?"

She turned up her face to look at me with eyes as meek and gentle as years ago and nodded.

8

The discovery of those three letters in Wei Shouyi's desk drawer set me thinking, and the more I thought about it, the deeper the tear in the reopened wound in my heart pulled, and the more agonizing the pain.

What a jerk he was! Stealing Qin Dujuan from me like that! I hated his duplicity and hypocrisy and I hated myself for being stupid and powerless.

I felt humiliation, regret, anger ...

And yet, my first order of business was to run around making all the arrangements for his funeral.

I forced myself to rationalize: This is a task assigned to me by the party organization. There is no room for personal feelings. It is not only a test of my generosity of spirit as a person, but also a tough test of my obedience to the party organization.

I went to the county civil affairs department a second time to inquire in detail about the provisions concerning death while on official duty. The woman cadre who received me said to me: It can be very simple; there must be a cause-and-effect relationship between the death and the official business. Let me give you some examples, "For instance if an engineer dies accidentally in the course of testing a new product, or a cadre is killed unexpectedly while arbitrating a dispute, or a teacher loses his life while taking his students on a spring outing ... all these deaths qualify as death while performing official duty."

I asked, "And if it's not simple, what factors could complicate matters?"

She replied, "Some people get it wrong. They often confuse death during working hours with death while on official duty. For example if someone who suffers from hypertension has an attack while watching TV at work and dies, it would be stretching it a bit to claim line-of-duty death with the civil affairs department."

I followed with another question, "If a cadre on an official business trip accidentally drives his car into a river and drowns on his way home in a dark night, can it be classified as a line-of-duty death?"

She flashed a smile at me and asked, "I think you are talking about Wei Shouyi. Am I right?"

I nodded, "How did you know?"

She said, "How many have died in a circumstance like that? He was the only one. News of his accident spread quickly in the county government."

I then asked, "In your view, does Wei Shouyi's death qualify as line-of-duty death?"

She said, "It involves several factors worth exploring. If it can be confirmed that his trip was indeed authorized by the party organization and his death was work-related—note that I've given some slack here because I did not mention the criterion of the causal relationship between the death and the official duty—then we can accept such a filing."

I inquired about the filing procedure and she gave a clear, detailed explanation.

After thanking her, I walked out of the civil affairs building. Once out the door I started thinking fast and furiously: Was that night trip of Wei Shouyi authorized by the party organization? Well, that's easy to fix. It only takes a nod from the Big Man and the approval of Party Secretary Shang, with his seal. That's confirmation enough. But to prove that his death was work-related would not be as easy. If Wei Shouyi drove while intoxicated that night and had a mysterious woman with him to boot, it would be even harder to claim line-of-duty death.

I admit that a very important reason for my painstaking effort to have Wei Shouyi's death classified as line-of-duty death was Qin Dujuan. Leaving aside the episode with Qin Dujuan in my past, even if it was the wife of any other cadre in the town government compound, I would gladly have made the same effort. This was a newly widowed, defenseless woman facing an uncertain future alone with nothing but tears! If the party did not try to help her, who would? Therefore, I tried not to take a single step or make a single inquiry without seeing the image of Qin Dujuan and her tear-reddened eyes floating before my eyes. I could not put my finger on exactly what my feelings for her were. But one thing was certain: After seeing those three letters hidden in Wei Shouyi's drawer, I had already forgiven her. She was not to blame for the failure of our relationship. I was the victim of a little scheme, and so was she.

I directed my steps toward the county traffic police brigade and found Qiu Sanbao.

I asked him, "How is the investigation into Town Chief Wei's accident going?"

Sanbao told me that the autopsy report was in, "The possibility of murder has been ruled out. He was indeed driving while intoxicated but he did not drink much. His blood had only a trace amount of alcohol."

I asked, "Have you clarified the question of the

shoe and the bra?"

Sanbao said, "There's a problem there. You see, once murder had been ruled out, the forensic police lost interest fast. I would not be surprised if the matter of the shoe and the bra is shelved."

I asked, "What do you mean shelved?"

Sanbao said, "It means it will die on the shelf. They don't actively pursue leads. The significance of the woman's shoe and bra is left to the imagination."

I said, "But that would leave the case unsolved."

Sanbao questioned me, "What do you mean unsolved? Do you have any idea how many such insignificant, minor cases are dropped for lack of evidence every year?"

I continued along my line of inquiry, "Then can our town government start arranging Town Chief Wei's funeral now? It's getting warmer; you can't continue putting him on ice for much longer."

Sanbao said, "Nobody is stopping you. Have your people come anytime to take him back."

Sanbao said it with a jarring nonchalance.

I asked in a whisper, "Shouyi's eulogy has not been finalized. Do you think I can write that he died in the performance of official duty?"

Sanbao pulled a sober face and said, "I'm not the

person to ask. I work for the traffic police, not the personnel department of the county party committee."

Casting a glance at Sanbao's smoke-yellowed face, I cursed in my heart: You sly bastard of a cop! Was it that hard to offer a hint?

As I aimlessly strolled in the streets of the county town, I was suddenly seized with a desire to go to the morgue of the traffic police brigade to look in on Wei Shouyi on his bed of ice. I hadn't taken a look at him after working on his case for all these days. As a colleague as well as in view of my mission in town, it stood to reason that I should pay him a visit.

I turned around and headed for Sanbao's office. I was sure that Sanbao was sick and tired of me by now. But that was the least of my concerns. It was only once in many years that someone in the town government died; he shouldn't complain too much if I, his old school buddy, sought his help under these circumstances. As I entered the building, it occurred to me that this would be a good time to get in touch with Qin Dujuan and ask her to bring some clean clothing for Wei Shouyi to wear on his trip to the beyond. I was told that Qin Dujuan had come a few days before to visit Wei Shouyi. Zhang Fulian, who accompanied her on the visit, said, "Qin

Dujuan is clearly an educated woman, she didn't go through any of the theatrics like foot-stamping or chest-thumping or cursing heaven and earth, but only quiet mourning, with soft sobbing and a hand over her mouth." At this characterization of Qin Dujuan, I wondered to myself what Zhang Fulian really understood about grieving.

As I made my way to the gatehouse to make a call, I looked up the phone number of the town school in my address book. The call went through but they were unable to get Qin Dujuan to take the call: she did not come to school, according to the person who came to the phone. I called her home but she wasn't there either. Where did she go? It wouldn't feel right if I went alone to see Wei Shouyi ...

Just as I was closing the address book, a line of fine characters scribbled on the last page jumped out at my eyes. They were written hastily in a fine hand with a ballpoint pen; I nearly jumped as if I had stepped on sharp spikes. The line read: On the afternoon of January 27 of the year xxxx, I borrowed 2,800 yuan from Wei Shouyi in the office. Don't forget to pay back.

I'll be damned! Not long before the Spring Festival, I was planning to buy a color TV, but the price of the new model that had just gone on sale at the county mall went over my budget, so I borrowed some money from Wei Shouyi. As time passed, I had somehow completely forgotten to pay him back!

I really messed up, I thought. I stamped my foot in frustration and was so rattled that I no longer felt in a mood to see Wei Shouyi at the morgue. The agitation in my mind caused a sudden constriction in my chest. I needed to make this right immediately. As I walked out of the building I kept cursing myself for not having the presence of mind to repay the loan at the earliest opportunity and when I still had a chance. Now I owed a debt to a dead man. How could I face the dead man at his memorial service?

Qin Dujuan came into my mind once more. I knew that the only remedy now was to pay that money back to Qin Dujuan. If I didn't acquit myself of this debt I would have no peace of mind.

I lost no time in renting a beat-up motorcycle and hurried back to our town to get some money. It was already night when I arrived in the compound and in the building only the Big Man's office had a light on. When I passed by his office I overheard an exchange that scared the wits out of me. I recognized the voices of Town Chief You Baida and Wang Shuangxi, the owner of Galloping Horses, Inc.

Wang Shuangxi was saying, "Big Man! Don't blame me; I did personally hand the money to Wei Shouyi ..."

The Big Man inquired icily, "When did you do that?"

Wang Shuangxi said, "I remember it clearly, it was last Wednesday! In a reserved banquet room at the Heavenly Aroma Restaurant!"

The Big Man continued, "And you gave him 420 thousand yuan?"

Wang Shuangxi answered, "Absolutely, 420 thousand! In cash! I made it very clear to Wei Shouyi that he was to give you 210 thousand."

The Big Man said spitefully, "210 thousand my foot! I didn't see a damned penny!"

Wang Shuangxi said, "Well, he died the next day before he had time to hand it to you! I gave him the money, that's the honest truth. If I lied, I'll be cursed with a watery death in the river, just like Wei Shouyi!"

The Big Man said, "Shush, shush, shush! I don't want you to curse yourself. Since you gave all the money to Wei Shouyi, he should be the one to take care of that business of yours. I'm washing my hands of it."

Wang Shuangxi nearly cried with despondence, "Big Man! That's so cruel of you! How can I make you believe me … Big Man! Please! Put Galloping Horses at the head of the list, if for nothing else, at least for the fact that we go back a long way, you and I …"

The Big Man impatiently interrupted Wang Shuangxi, "Where do you think Wei Shouyi kept the 420 thousand yuan?"

Wang Shuangxi said, "Most probably in his home. It's safer there."

The Big Man said, "That's bull. I know he had a mistress."

Wang Shuangxi said, "Then it must be kept in his office. Can you open his desk drawer to take a look?"

The Big Man said, "How can I open it without authorization? Only his wife has access to his personal stuff."

Wang Shuangxi asked, "Has his wife been to his office?"

The Big Man answered impatiently, "How would I know? According to Ah Peng, Wei Shouyi's keys have been turned over to the party committee for safekeeping. They are with the Old Whip …"

My heart started to race.

Then I heard Wang Shuangxi say, "Big Man! I've

an idea: Let's pry open Wei Shouyi's drawer tonight! What the heck!"

The Big Man did not say anything; the only sound was of his hand slapping his head ...

A cold breeze blew in, setting my hair on end. An owl hooted in the ancient camphor laurels; its cries sounded like a baby wailing in the night. On the Tongchao River outside the compound wall, boats sailed by, leaving behind the squeaking sound of oars and the uninhibited, loud conversation of the boatmen. The barking of dogs far and near accentuated the deathly quiet of this rustic country far from the main county town.

I tiptoed past in the corridor and went into my office, got out all the cash in my drawer, about three or four thousand yuan, and exited the town government building at the other end of the corridor.

I immediately dialed Party Secretary Shang's number.

As soon as he answered I said, "On the way to my office a moment ago I overheard the Big Man and Wang Shuangxi discussing something important. They said they were going to pry open Wei Shouyi's drawer tonight!"

Alarmed, Party Secretary Shang asked in a

lowered voice, "Are you sure you heard it right?"

I said in a similar tone, "Without a shadow of a doubt!"

Party Secretary Shang asked, "Did they say why they wanted to pry open the drawer?"

After considering the question, I said, "I didn't hear them clearly."

Party Secretary Shang went on to ask. "Do you still have Wei Shouyi's keys?"

I said, "Yes. The Big Man asked me for them, but I did not give them to him."

After a brief silence, he said, "Okay, I understand."

I asked him one more question, "Do you want me to discuss with you in person what to do next?"

Party Secretary Shang said, "I'll take the matter in hand. I want you to stay out of it."

Before I could say anything, he hung up.

That was Party Secretary Shang's style. He would not allow anyone to share any crucial decision-making with him. He had an oligarchic style of taking sole control of the situation at hand. At such moments, he had an intimidating presence. I could picture him lighting a cigarette after hanging up and fixing his eyes on some lamp outside the window while hatching an airtight plan for the evening, with all the contingencies taken into consideration. I wondered how the Old Whip was going to strike the decisive blow that night.

I became excited despite myself. I suspected that in the next few hours Party Secretary Shang would map out his strategy, based on the information I'd provided, and muster his forces to deal a fatal blow to his old rival. Would he alert Captain Xu of the police station to lay an ambush in the compound with his elite team? Or maybe he would personally lead a team of trusted subordinates in a surprise raid that would catch Wang Shuangxi and the Big Man in the act of prying open the drawer. No matter what, I could foresee drama unfolding that night in the town government compound.

After speaking to Party Secretary Shang on the phone, I made a call to Qin Dujuan. I was anxious to repay that money. I told her on the phone, "I need to speak to you on an urgent matter. Could I come to your place?"

Qin Dujuan explained, "A relative of ours is here to discuss Wei Shouyi's funeral arrangements. Let me go over to your place when I can get away."

I said "Okay" and went to the Old Tongxing Restaurant in town to get some take-away noodle soup and a few marinated dishes. I went back home to wait while I ate.

It was past 10 in the evening when Qin Dujuan arrived.

She was coming to my place for the first time. The moment she walked in, her eyes made a quick survey of my small, bare two-room apartment—one single bed, a desk, a fridge, a color TV, and a cold, rarely used stove. I seemed to detect a twitch on one side of her face.

I motioned her to a chair and made her a cup of tea.

She said, "Is this how you have lived all these years?"

I said with a chuckle, "Why? Is there anything wrong with it?"

Her eyes reddened as she said, "How can you say that ...?"

I knew that I sounded a little irreverent and cynical and that she truly felt sorry for me. But was there any other way to reply to her question?

After a long silence, she asked, "Since your divorce have you ever given thought to remarrying?"

I finished my noodle soup and stuffed the leftover food into the refrigerator. I said, "Let's not talk about that. I wanted to speak to you about two important matters."

She looked at me, a little alarmed.

I produced an envelope prepared in advance and said, "Here's 2,800 yuan, which I borrowed from Shouyi shortly before the Spring Festival, in order to buy this TV that you see. Who'd have thought ... Now I can only pay it back to you. Count it."

Qin Dujuan cast a quick sidelong glance at the envelope and said, "Why don't we forget about it?"

I said, "How can I do that? Debt has to be repaid even if the creditor is dead."

I realized only after the words were out of my mouth that they could be interpreted in a different light. But I was sure that Qin Dujuan understood what I meant. I forced the envelope into her hand.

Qin Dujuan lifted the envelope and took a look at it. She said, "You seem to be determined to repay your debt to Wei Shouyi. What about Wei Shouyi's debt to you? Shouldn't it be repaid also?"

I was at a loss to answer that. I now realized she had misconstrued my words.

Seeing that I was not replying, she said emphatically, "If you are repaying a debt owed to a person who is now dead, then I see no reason why debt incurred by Wei Shouyi while he was alive shouldn't be repaid."

I asked, "What debt did he owe?"

She said, "He owed you, Teacher Peng."

I pleaded, "Don't say that."

She said, "He intercepted three letters I wrote to you. That was a debt he owed not only you, but also to me. He owed us a life together!"

I lifted my head in astonishment. Qin Dujuan's eyes held mine; the trembling tears could not obscure a fiery ardor in them. Her face was pale and anemic, and under the electric light almost took on translucence. I had never before seen in her, this woman not yet 30 years of age, such hatred toward a person, especially given that person happened to be her late husband!

She continued, "That day when I got home I began thinking about it. If he had not intercepted the three letters, you and I would perhaps have ended up united, and we would have had a life together ..."

The sharp jabs of pain in my heart returned. I said, "All that happened many years ago. It's water under the bridge. Let's not talk about it."

After another brief silence she said, "And that four hundred thousand yuan and more! I doubt that it's clean money. It is in Wei Shouyi's custody, but most probably he owed something to somebody."

I marveled to myself, "What a keen eye this woman's got!"

I said, "Now that you bring that up, the second matter I wanted to discuss was the money." A nervous look came over her face.

I said, "I'll be straight with you, Qin Dujuan. The 420 thousand yuan is indeed shady money. I only found out tonight. It is 'facilitation money' given by Wang Shuangxi, owner of Galloping Horses Developers, Inc., to the Big Man and Shouyi. Wang Shuangxi does not easily part with money unless he expects to reap big benefits in exchange. By shelling out the 420 thousand yuan, he must expect the Big Man and Shouyi to render him a service—let's not get into the specifics of it. They had not reckoned that Shouyi's sudden death, turned the facilitation money into a one-way transaction—the deal was brought to an abrupt end with Shouyi's passing!"

Qin Dujuan said, "Wang Shuangxi has worked hard for his money; I should return the money to him."

I shot to my feet, frightening Qin Dujuan, who flinched.

I said, "I can't imagine anyone else doing a thing like that! Do you think they will all become model citizens when you return this money to Wang Shuangxi? And that you would be rewarded for your good will?"

Qin Dujuan said, "I don't expect to be rewarded; I just want peace of mind."

I said in a loud voice, "What's there to lose your peace of mind over? Why should you feel uneasy? What's 420 thousand yuan to Wang Shuangxi? A pittance! One hair out of a million on a cow's body! He builds hundreds, thousands of apartments a year, and for your information, the profit he makes on one apartment alone is more than 420 thousand!"

Qin Dujuan said coolly, "It's his business if he makes a huge profit, but I can't take his money just because he makes a handsome profit."

I said, "If you insist on returning the money, nothing I say can stop you. But I want you to know that during all these years Wei Shouyi had done a great deal to facilitate matters for Wang Shuangxi. With Wei Shouyi's help, Wang Shuangxi made a good deal more than four million, even forty million yuan. Do you really want to hand the 420 thousand yuan over to this corrupt man?"

Qin Dujuan said, with her eyes on me, "Are you suggesting ...?"

I said, "You keep the money for now and don't tell anybody about it. If Wang Shuangxi, or the Big Man, or anybody else asks you about it, just give the uniform answer 'I know nothing.' Money is money and will come in handy someday."

She nodded, but I could see that the consent was given with great reluctance.

9

The next morning I intentionally stayed away from the town government compound. I knew all hell must have broken loose there and Party Secretary Shang must have taken some bold, earth-shaking action during the night. I was in no hurry to make any inquiry about it. I needed to give a wide berth to the compound for now to avoid drawing suspicion on myself. As for what kind of hell was let loose in the town government, someone was bound to bring the story to me soon enough, and with juicy details.

I told Qin Dujuan to bring a complete set of clothing for Wei Shouyi's last trip and I accompanied her to the county town. We visited Wei Shouyi in the low building behind the traffic police headquarters.

Wei Shouyi lay in solitude on a steel bed placed in the middle of the bare room. He was wearing his usual outfit, a coffee-colored jacket, navy blue dress slacks, shirt and tie, except that the knot in the tie was askew, leather shoes and white socks on his feet. The attire was mud-besmirched in multiple spots and had not been changed since he was pulled out of the river by Sanbao. The thought that this soggy outfit had stuck to his skin for so many days sent a shiver through my body and chilled my heart.

He lay rigid. His eyes were not completely closed and the half-drawn eyelids revealed a lifeless stare. His face was white as a sheet, its skin diaphanous and shiny, as if a jab of the finger would pierce it. His body was somewhat swollen and his facial features had an unfamiliar look. Especially disconcerting was his mouth, which gaped skyward, presenting an ominous-looking black hole. The sight of that mouth convinced me that Wei Shouyi must have struggled desperately in his last moments. The final expression frozen on his face was one of anger, pain and a kind of wry resignation.

A chilly wind crept up and slammed shut the

steel door behind us. Caught off guard by the sudden bang, both Qin Dujuan and I blanched with fright and we lifted our heads to exchange a look.

I walked over to the door and secured it. Qin Dujuan was sobbing into her hands. She murmured indistinct words in front of the body. We stood silently at Shouyi's side for a long moment. Then we filed all the necessary papers with the traffic police and ordered a hearse from the county funeral home.

The hearse was a black minivan, which had reportedly been bought by someone dispatched by the county civil affairs department to Shanghai for that express purpose, and refitted and painted at the factory.

The funeral home employee and the chauffeur got out of the hearse and walked around the morgue bed once; then they placed a stretcher on the floor and moved Shouyi over to the stretcher, on which was prepositioned a body bag. Once Wei Shouyi was on the stretcher, the funeral home employee zipped up the bag to enclose the body. I saw Qin Dujuan stretch out her hands for a second; I did not know what she intended to do, but I knew she was struggling within herself.

The employee asked, "Do you want to keep his old clothes when we are done preparing him?"

Qin Dujuan said no.

The employee's next question was, "When do you want to schedule the ceremony?"

I told him it had yet to be decided and that the matter would be discussed by the town government.

The employee said, "When the date is set, be sure to call us. We are having a busy season, so if the reservation is not made well in advance, you may not get a ceremonial hall in time."

The mortuary employee had a kindly face and a friendly manner of speech; when he moved Shouyi together with the chauffeur he exhibited great care and respect. I was quite touched by it and offered them a 100-yuan note in token of our thanks. With a smile and a shake of their heads, he and the chauffeur declined and left.

When she saw the hearse leave in a cloud of dust, Qin Dujuan began to grieve in earnest. She gripped my arm and leaned on me and began to sob unrestrainedly. Her hand digging into my skin was shaking violently.

I said, "Teacher Qin, don't take it too hard. Your health is more important."

Qin Dujuan said, "I feel so sorry for him. He was only 37."

I said, "Who would have guessed? You must take

it in stride."

Qin Dujuan said, "I saw that agonized expression on his face. Do you think he will look better after the mortician is done making him up?"

I said, "He should look better."

Qin Dujuan asked, "Can his mouth be closed?"

I said I would talk to the mortuary as soon as I could.

We walked a distance in the downtown street, with me holding her arm, before we hailed a motorized tricycle, which took us back to Tacheng after a bumpy ride, with motor sputtering and loose parts rattling. When we arrived at the intersection where she was supposed to get off, Qin Dujuan showed no sign of moving. I realized then that she had fallen fast asleep against my shoulder. Looking at her tousled hair and haggard face, I sighed and thought: Wei Shouyi! How you've wronged her!

I went that afternoon to the town government compound. On the way I was secretly expecting a spectacle and relished the thought. I went first to seek out Old Ding the gate man in the hope of finding out about any new developments. But Old Ding was all serenity. I thought: Party Secretary Shang is an old hand after all. He must have succeeded in limiting the damage to the minimum.

The moment I walked into the office, Party Secretary Shang called me to his office.

Party Secretary Shang said, "How is the matter of Wei Shouyi proceeding?"

I gave him an account of my dealings with various authorities in the county government, of the female articles discovered by the police in the car, and of the investigation ending without any conclusion.

Party Secretary Shang asked, "What's your take on the items found in the car?"

I said, "They can't be a good thing. But Wei Shouyi is dead, what can be done about them? I don't see any good coming out of getting to the bottom of it; that might drag the name of Wei Shouyi through the mud. What do you say, Party Secretary Shang?"

Party Secretary Shang said after a brief reflection, "I'm inclined to agree."

I had been waiting for Party Secretary Shang to bring up the matter of the previous night, but he mentioned not a word about it and steered the discussion toward the date of Wei Shouyi's burial and other related matters that needed to be attended to. Finally the discussion turned to the mention of line-of-duty death in the eulogy text.

I briefed him on what had happened during my visit to the county civil affairs department. I said, "Town Chief You wants to classify Wei Shouyi's death as line-of-duty, so I think we can ignore the criteria of the county civil affairs department. The town government can make its own determination. It's not too late to alter the conclusion if circumstances require it in the future. Didn't Kang Sheng, that evil central government leader, eventually have his grave removed from the prestigious Babaoshan Cemetery for revolutionary heroes even though he was buried with full honors?"

Party Secretary Shang said, "You mean there are issues with Wei Shouyi, but that they have yet to be uncovered?"

I hastened to say, "No, that wasn't what I meant at all! I was only giving an example. I have come to the view that it is quite pointless to obsess about the line-of-duty death issue. Given that Wei Shouyi did a great service to our town in life and died in such a tragic manner, I have no objection to classifying it as death in the line of duty."

Without saying a word, Party Secretary Shang got up and started pacing about the office. He smoked a cigarette with knitted eyebrows and finally said, "That's how we'll proceed, for now."

With that, he lowered his voice to tell me something else, "In the operation to catch our thieves last night, they were alerted, so it ended in failure."

I asked in alarm, "How did that happen? Was my information inaccurate?"

Party Secretary Shang said, "The information was perfectly accurate, the problem was I ..." Shaking his head, he extinguished his cigarette and lit another.

"I'm not so sure now about the loyalty of this Captain Xu of the police station. After my conversation with you on the phone I went in person to the police station and gave instructions to Captain Xu to deploy his team with a view to catching the burglars red-handed. I told him I wanted to join the all-night stakeout. But the fellow said, 'Why would you, Party Secretary Shang, want to run the risk of catching a cold in an all-night stakeout? Am I that useless in your eyes? As long as the information is reliable, I promise I'll catch the burglars with my own hands and then, Party Secretary Shang, you can reward me for a job well done!' So I went back to wait for his phone call. Finally the call came, but it was to say that two members of the joint civil defense force had been deployed to keep watch under a box tree, but it so happened that the Big Man and Wang Shuangxi emerged from the office and from above, pissed onto the tree while looking at the starry sky. When the hot piss landed on their heads, the two members of the joint civil defense force let out a startled cry, thus instantly giving themselves away. The Big Man summoned Captain Xu and took him to task, asking him if these people were out to steal state secrets. So the whole thing fell flat."

I said with great disappointment, "Luck is not on our side. There's nothing we can do."

Party Secretary Shang said, "I have a suspicion that this fellow Captain Xu had some secret alliance with the Big Man. I deeply regret not having taken charge myself last night."

I said, "Sooner or later they will get caught. We'll wait and see."

Party Secretary Shang agreed. "It's as well. When you have a secret adversary on your team, you learn to be more careful. That's the upside of this mess. What do you say?"

With a rueful chuckle I nodded.

Wei Shouyi's funeral was scheduled for April 30th. On

the 28th, I made a special trip to the county funeral home to check Wei Shouyi's facial preparation. In a big hall lined with bodies, I met the same mortuary employee who came to the traffic police morgue to pick up the body. We greeted each other like old friends. I offered him a Zhonghua cigarette and stuffed a pack of them into his pocket.

The employee said, "It's nice of you to pay another visit to Town Chief Wei."

I told him we had been colleagues for many years.

He told me a woman comrade had been there a little while before to see Town Chief Wei.

I asked, "Was it the wife of Town Chief Wei, the one you met at the traffic police brigade?"

The employee said, "No, this woman was taller and her arm was in a sling. She also had some facial injuries ..."

I tensed and immediately thought of the female articles found in the crashed car.

The employee said, "The woman comrade didn't say a word or shed a tear, but only stood at Town Chief Wei's bedside briefly before leaving."

I asked anxiously, "Did she say where she was from?"

The employee shook his head.

I asked, "Does anyone on the staff know her?"

The employee again shook his head.

When I walked out of the funeral home, I realized that my armpits were dripping with cold sweat …

Back in my apartment, Town Chief You Baida, who had sent his secretary Little Ye to fetch me, urgently summoned me to a meeting at the town government building.

Taking down a copy of the day's provincial newspaper from the newspaper rack, Town Chief You said, "Ah Peng! Look at this—"

It was a headline piece about the ten best town and village chiefs of the province, and Wei Shouyi was rated number one! The photo accompanying the article was a copy of the same one that I burned the other night in the office.

I said to the Big Man, "The editor of the provincial paper was not thinking. He should have added a black border to Shouyi's photo."

The Big Man said, "It's you, Ah Peng, who are not thinking. The provincial government is treating the announcement of the ten best town and village chiefs as a festive event. The addition of a black border would jinx it for them."

I said, "Maybe the provincial government is unaware of Wei Shouyi's accident."

The Big Man said, "Well, the provincial capital is a great distance from us. Let's not talk about this. I sent for you because I want you to take this paper and pay another visit to the county civil affairs department. Tell them this: Town Chief Wei has been rated among the ten best town and village chiefs of the province. Are you still refusing to certify his death as line-of-duty? Make sure they give swift approval so that when the town government gives the eulogy at the funeral the day after tomorrow, we have the official green light to refer to it as death in the line of duty."

I said, "Yes, I'm on it."

The Audi for the exclusive use of the top leadership was already idling at the entrance of the town government building. When I went into my office to get my briefcase I heard the phone ring. When I picked up the phone, my hair suddenly stood on end.

The female voice out of the handset, trembling and undulating, sounded as if it had floated down from the sky, or had risen from a cavern fathoms deep.

She asked, "Are you Town Chief Peng?"

I asked, "Who is this?"

The woman said, "You don't know me but I know you. I often heard Wei Shouyi talk about you. I preceded you this morning at the mortuary to see Wei Shouyi ... actually I saw you at the entrance."

I muttered an acknowledgment and remembered once more the woman's shoe and the bra. And I vaguely recalled having heard this voice somewhere ...

The woman said, "Town Chief Peng, I heard that you were on very good terms with Wei Shouyi."

I said, "We were friends for many long years."

The woman said, "I also heard you've worked hard to get his death certified as a death in the line-of-duty."

I said, "Yes, I worked reasonably hard."

Then it hit me! Yes! It was this woman's voice I heard on those occasions when I picked up calls intended for Wei Shouyi in our office. Obviously this was Wei Shouyi's lover!

The woman suddenly said with a sinister laugh, "Town Chief Peng, heed my advice: Don't bother trying too hard. I alone in this world know Wei Shouyi died a less than noble death that night. Do you know where he went that night? And whom he was with? I'll tell you: that night Wei Shouyi stayed at the Tianlu Hotel, with me; we drank and I slept with him ..."

I asked if she could give me her name.

The woman said, "It seems you, Town Chief Peng, are also interested in getting acquainted with me."

I mustered enough courage to say, "Why don't we meet?"

The woman said she would meet me on one condition.

I said, "Fine, go ahead and state your condition."

The woman said, "That night Wei Shouyi was driving back to his office to get a certain amount of cash for me when the accident occurred. I know that you picked up Wei Shouyi's personal effects and the key to his office drawer should be among them ..."

I said, "You are right."

The woman said, "I'd trouble you to get the cash from Wei Shouyi's drawer and turn it over to me."

I asked, "How much does he have in his drawer?"

The woman said, "420 thousand yuan."

I was astounded; I thought of what Qin Dujuan did that night, her hands on the drawer.

I asked the woman, "Did Town Chief Wei mention where he got the money?"

The woman said, "That's none of my business."

My hand tightened around the phone and my palm began to sweat profusely.

The woman said, "Town Chief Peng, I'm not asking you to open that drawer without compensation ..."

I asked her what she meant.

The woman answered, "Once you open the drawer and deliver the cash into my hand, I will immediately pay you 100 thousand yuan for your trouble."

I wouldn't listen anymore but calmly put the phone back on its cradle.

On the day of Wei Shouyi's funeral, I suddenly and unaccountably lost my voice and therefore missed the chance to preside over the final ceremony in honor of my old friend. I stood not far from Wei Shouyi's body and saw that his mouth remained agape, like a deep, dark hole. I felt guilty about this gaping hole, for I had failed to do a satisfactory job of arranging Wei Shouyi's posthumous affairs. I was so guilt-ridden that I dared not look Qin Dujuan in the eye.

The memorial service was presided over by Party Secretary Shang in my stead (thus raising the ranking of the service), and Town Chief You Baida read the eulogy. I saw the Big Man publicly wipe off his tears with an upward movement of the fat heel of his thumb and I heard him read out the words "the good town chief of the people, Wei Shouyi ... tragic death ... while performing official duty."

I surveyed unobtrusively the surroundings in the hope of spotting a woman with an arm in a sling and a disfigured face. I thought she might be standing quietly in some corner wearing a bandage and dark sunglasses. But I did not see her anywhere.

One night a few days after the ceremony, Qin Dujuan came to my apartment. The moment she saw me, she asked, "Teacher Peng, why have you grown more white hair?"

I said, "Have I?"

I looked at myself in the mirror and discovered to my astonishment that half of my hair had turned white. It was a stranger I was seeing in the mirror! My heart sank.

I asked Qin Dujuan, "Has something come up?"

She said, "According to the local custom of the town, I should go to the scene of the accident to call back his spirit. Do you know the location?"

I nodded.

At dawn the next morning, by the river near the 12-kilometer mark on the County Road, two voices—one male and one female—were heard calling in all directions, "Wei Shouyi—Wei Shouyi—"

The female voice was plaintive and low, the male voice rough and loud.

On the sand bank, smoke curled up slowly from the burning paper.

In the mist that hung in the air like gray gauze, a cuckoo started to call. Its singing rose and fell as it flew hither and thither, becoming mingled with the male and female voices raised to call back the spirit of the dead—

Cuckoo, cuckoo, cuckoo, cuckoo ...

The Boarding Students

1

In the refectory of Huanglou Township Secondary School, upwards of a hundred students were slurping their porridge. They ate on their feet, in silence, except for the awe-inspiring chorus of gurgling as hot gruel rolled down the hundred or so gullets at the same time.

Luo Zhaoying's table was situated near the northeast corner of the refectory. She was appointed head of the table. She had a dainty way of holding her rice bowl with the slender fingers of her left hand, white and made almost translucent by the sun's rays. The thumb and the middle finger held the side of the enamel bowl in an arc, the index finger sticking up in a hook to secure the bowl, and the pinky and the ring finger wrapped around the bowl, forming an orchid-like pattern. Every time Ma Xiaolong saw her hand in this position, he couldn't stop himself from wondering what it was about this girl that made her smallest gesture such a feast for the eyes.

Ma Xiaolong was still staring in fascination at her hand when Luo Zhaoying suddenly turned her head and said with an anxious expression in her face, "Principal Ma was looking for you."

Ma Xiaolong said, "Really?"

Luo Zhaoying said, "He told me when he ran into me at the school entrance."

Ma Xiaolong asked, "What did he want with me, do you know?"

Luo Zhaoying said, "Who knows?"

Ma Xiaolong realized that in all the years he had been in school this was the first time a school principal wanted to talk to him. He knew that it never boded well when the principal asked for you. The news made him anxious.

Ma was actually not the surname of the principal. He was given this sobriquet, behind his back, because his face was covered with *ma zi*, or pockmarks. Ma Xiaolong disliked the principal, not because of his revulsion to the pockmarks, but because of the frequency of the principal's visits to the school doctor's office to see Zheng Xiuli, who was the wife of Ma Xiaolong's father's younger brother. Ma Xiaolong felt humiliated by these visits. Ma Xiaolong's aunt, Zheng Xiuli, was the school doctor, and was considered the prettiest among the female faculty. On each visit Principal Pockmark would stay in the doctor's office a long time and receive treatment for an undisclosed illness behind a securely locked door. Ma Xiaolong knew for a fact that his aunt detested Principal Pockmark but would flash a radiant smile at him in public. Ma Xiaolong was puzzled by his aunt's behavior.

Ma Xiaolong was one of the shortest in his class, so that in physical education he would be relegated to the back rows of any formation. Academically however he was at the forefront of the class. In all subjects—math, physics, chemistry, reading, history, and geography—he consistently ranked in the top three. He also had beautiful handwriting and he won the Ninth Grade table tennis championship. His Achilles' heel was his bad pedigree, politically speaking. This weakness did not manifest itself in his academic work or when he played ping pong, but was evident when he interacted with people. He would always stay at the back of crowds, back hunched and chest drawn in, listening attentively and timidly to what was being said. He rarely looked people in their eye, and when he did, it was only for the briefest moment before his eyes moved quickly away as if in fear of being burned.

Luo Zhaoying said to him, "It's ridiculous that you are called Xiaolong (little dragon). There's not an iota of the *long* (dragon) in you as far as I can see." Ma Xiaolong responded with a sheepish smile. He admitted he was not a dragon type, but rather a fish nursing an invisible wound swimming close to the edge of the water.

Luo Zhaoying continued, "There is going to be a morning assembly of the entire school after breakfast."

Ma Xiaolong was startled by the announcement and his eyes looked over the rim of his enamel bowl to fix on Luo Zhaoying. The weekly morning assembly of the entire school normally fell on a Friday and it was only Wednesday. It occurred to Ma Xiaolong that something must have happened for the school to reschedule the convocation.

He asked, "What's going to be discussed at the assembly?"

Luo Zhaoying said, "I don't know."

As she uttered these words, she quietly poured some of her porridge into Ma Xiaolong's bowl. Ma Xiaolong said "You need this yourself." Luo Zhaoying said, "I'm already full." Ma Xiaolong said, "How can you be full? Everyone got only one ladleful of porridge." Luo Zhaoying said, "I am full. You boys have a larger appetite, go ahead and eat it."

As the bowl of porridge see-sawed between the two, an enamel bowl the size of a small wash basin was thrust under their nose, followed by a loud voice, "Don't be modest! You have some spare porridge? Let me have it!"

Ma Xiaolong and Luo Zhaoying looked briefly at the bowl and exchanged a glance but did not say a word. That brief look at the proffered bowl told them it was Liu Tingsong coming to cadge table scraps. Liu Tingsong was, like them, a student in Class 6 of Ninth Grade. He was tall and burly, and had an insatiable appetite, and always had his hand out for any food other students could spare. There was a quiver of the bowl in Ma Xiaolong's hand, but Luo Zhaoying immediately checked his impulse with a glance, and the basin-sized bowl Liu Tingsong held out was kept suspended in midair, waiting. Ma Xiaolong looked timidly from Luo Zhaoying to Liu Tingsong, and finally went ahead and poured some of his porridge into that big bowl.

Luo Zhaoying gave Ma Xiaolong a withering sidelong glance.

Liu Tingsong brought the bowl to his mouth, tilted it at a right angle and slurped up its content, making an exaggeratedly loud noise as he did so. Then he moved the bowl away from his mouth and looked with a wicked air from Ma Xiaolong to Luo Zhaoying. She angrily turned her back to him, her mouth twisted into a barely audible curse.

All the students assigned to this table were boarders in Class 6 of Ninth Grade. Liu Tingsong and Ma Xiaolong shared a room and slept in opposite bunks in the boys' dormitory. According to the rule of co-ed seating at the refectory, they—one girl and two boys—and Fan Yuling, another girl student, were assigned to this table to take their meals. On this day, however, Fan Yuling was not present at the table. She had to be taken to the clinic in town, after having fainted from hunger the day before during morning exercise. Two more girl students collapsed after her. Zheng Xiuli, Ma Xiaolong's aunt, spent an entire day dealing with the aftermath; the town doctor had had to be called in. The unfortunate incident was more or less laid to rest in the afternoon when all three girls were taken to the town clinic for observation.

Needless to say, Liu Tingsong ate Fan Yuling's meal.

Liu Tingsong was unpopular in school. He was equally disliked by fellow students and faculty, as well as the chief cook of the refectory, who was put off by his gluttony and tendency to hog food. His family was actually comfortably off; his parents, both of whom were cadres serving in the town government, supplied him with plenty of snacks on their frequent visits, but his craving for food never seemed satisfied and he was forever hungry for more. His table manners were terrible; he slurped and smacked like a pig. One of the many reasons he invented to justify his demand for a larger portion of food, and which he often cited at the table, was that girls, like little hens with tiny craws, can't eat much and should have their portion cut so that the boys get a larger portion. Luo Zhaoying and Fan Yuling were so deeply resentful of his arguments that they decided to snub him. They would only give Ma Xiaolong food if they had any to spare. This had the effect of making Liu Tingsong take out his anger on Ma Xiaolong, accusing Ma Xiaolong of ingratiating himself with the girls and causing Liu's isolation. Feeling emboldened by his burly build and good political pedigree, he made it his business to pick on Ma Xiaolong.

Another reason for Liu Tingsong's resentment

and jealousy of Ma Xiaolong was his closeness to Luo Zhaoying.

Luo Zhaoying was the prettiest girl in Class 6 of Ninth Grade, if not in the entire Ninth Grade. When boys gathered and had nothing better to do, they would discuss and rate the girls on the basis of their looks. Every girl in the school had been ranked. Of the more than one hundred girls in Ninth Grade, there were a dozen considered pretty and their names were bandied about among the boys. While their rankings varied, Luo Zhaoying was the only one to win unanimous approval and praise. Her rating was the highest and it was not uncommon for her to get the perfect score several times in a row. The boys gave her high marks because in addition to good looks, a delightful figure and a fair complexion, she had an air and a demeanor that set her apart from the other girls. She looked less like a girl born to a peasant family than one from an urban educated family.

Liu Tingsong did badly at his school work but was full of mischievous ideas. As early as in Seventh and Eighth Grade, he already started thinking of dating Luo Zhaoying. In Ninth Grade, with the adolescent height spurt, an enlarged Adam's apple, the appearance of stubble on his chin and the breakout of pimples across his face, came an irresistible attraction to girls and an even stronger urge to get Luo Zhaoying to become his date. One day a letter mailed through the post was delivered into Luo Zhaoying's hands at the school gate. When she opened the envelope she found to her surprise a love letter addressed to her by Liu Tingsong. She flushed furiously after a cursory glance at it, and fled into the safety of her dorm. Her first reaction was to tear it up but on second thought she decided not to give any false hope to Liu Tingsong. So she picked up a pen and wrote across his letter the two bold words "Keep dreaming!!!" adding the three exclamation points for good measure. She dropped the letter in Liu Tingsong's desk in the classroom.

When Liu Tingsong found his love letter returned, his face turned white and red with humiliation and annoyance. He gnashed his teeth and tore up the letter; as he was going to throw the fragments into the latrine, he happened to see, at the other end of the corridor, Luo Zhaoying and Ma Xiaolong in quiet conversation, which was punctuated by occasional bursts of laughter. This scene was forever etched in his mind as he thought: No wonder this girl doesn't like me. She's already dating Ma Xiaolong! It's even possible that Luo Zhaoying returned his letter on the advice of this bastard!

This incident had the effect of intensifying Liu Tingsong's animosity toward Ma Xiaolong. He gave Ma Xiaolong a hard time at every opportunity and devised devious ways of persecuting him.

Ma Xiaolong, however, was clueless about the real reason for Liu Tingsong's animus toward him, attributing it to Liu's bad temper. He suppressed his anger and studied doubly hard, thinking: I can't fight you, but at least I can avoid you. I'll earn good grade points and get myself admitted to a magnet high school. When I achieve that, Liu Tingsong, you'll no longer have me as your whipping boy!

So Ma Xiaolong plunged into his books, shutting out all other concerns. In Ninth Grade he was already studying math, physics and chemistry at the level of a high school senior. Once his math teacher Mr. Zhang wrote out a problem that filled half of the blackboard, saying it figured in the national college entrance examination of a certain year and he just wanted the students to have a foretaste of what they might expect in future exams. When he finished writing and put down the chalk he turned to face the class only to see blank stares from the dozens of students. It was then that Ma Xiaolong raised his hand and uttered the two words: no solution. Mr. Zhang asked, "How did you come to this conclusion?" Ma Xiaolong went up to the board and wrote a string of equations before fleeing back to his seat. After examining the equations, Mr. Zhang kept repeating, "Who'd have thought! Who'd have thought! Even a high school senior might not be able to give such an elegant answer."

The better Ma Xiaolong's academic performance, the bitterer Liu Tingsong's resentment of him grew. That morning, after breakfast, Luo Zhaoying said to Ma Xiaolong, "Let's go visit Fan Yuling at the town clinic during lunch break. What do you say?"

Looking cautiously around him, Ma Xiaolong said, "All right."

Luo Zhaoying said, "But let's remember to bring her something to eat."

Ma Xiaolong said, "My aunt gave me some fruit candies. I'll bring those."

Luo Zhaoying said, "Good. I have some biscuits. My biscuits and your fruit candies make a nice present."

Ma Xiaolong said, "We should leave right after lunch, otherwise we might not be back in time for the afternoon classes."

Luo Zhaoying said. "I'll wait for you at the usual place."

Ma Xiaolong nodded and felt an unaccountable warming in his chest as he watched Luo Zhaoying turn and walk away. This little secret between them caused a wild flutter in his adolescent heart.

The morning assembly was held, as usual, on the sport field. At the sound of the bell, the classes took their assigned positions in an orderly fashion. But surprisingly the students' marching in was not accompanied by the usual, familiar refrains of the *March of the Chinese People's Liberation Army*: "Forward, forward, forward, our troops march toward the sun." A whispered discussion rippled across the gathering as it grappled with this anomaly. Liu Tingsong asked pointblank his class teacher Jin Hexiang, a male teacher whose hair had grayed prematurely, "Teacher Jin, why aren't they playing the march today?"

Teacher Jin gave him a blank stare instead of an answer.

In Ma Xiaolong's estimation, there must have been a faculty meeting beforehand and there would be an announcement of grave import to be made at the assembly. Remembering Luo Zhaoying's relayed message that Principal Pockmark had been looking for him, he felt a sinking of his heart. He had a bad political pedigree because his father was once an army doctor in Kuomintang troops. For this reason he had never been able to hold up his head in school and he lived in constant apprehension. He was apt to imagine terrible things whenever there was a departure from routine; once bitten twice shy.

A mystified silence fell on faculty and students as the classes filed into the sports field, in a scattering of steps on the coal-dust paved tracks.

Principal Pockmark ascended the dais, his hand gripping a mike and his eyes making a sweep of the hundreds of students and faculty assembled on the athletic field. He coughed and boomed out the words, "I'd like to share some information with you on two matters today. The first is that for some time now a number of our students have fainted in class or on the athletic field during morning exercise and physical education sessions. You already know the reason for these fainting episodes; our country has been hit by natural disasters, which have resulted in poor harvests and food shortages, and as a consequence, serious malnutrition among our student body. Today there is further bad news from the town clinic. Fan Yuling, of Class 6 of Ninth Grade, who fainted yesterday on the athletic field, passed away about 4 o'clock this morning, after the doctors were unsuccessful in their rescue efforts ..."

A chorus of cries of disbelief went up from the hundreds of students.

There were none more dumbfounded than the students in Class 6 of Ninth Grade. They couldn't believe that the standard bearer in math who was sitting with them in the same classroom only recently had died. And in Class 6, it was Luo Zhaoying and Ma Xiaolong who took the news the hardest. Only a quarter of an hour before, they were talking about visiting Fan Yuling at the clinic during lunch break. They could not imagine that Fan Yuling, who shared their table at meal times, would never come back. For these two young souls, it was the first time death had come so close to home. They were blindsided by it.

The collective eyes of the gathering turned to Class 6 of Ninth Grade. A buzz of anxious inquiries and discussions hovered above the field.

Ma Xiaolong saw Luo Zhaoying glance at him over her shoulder. It was a glance fraught with disbelief, sorrow and pain. He saw her eyes brim with tears.

Here and there girls started to sob quietly and in a subdued way.

Principal Pockmark continued, after another cough, "This is the second student death at Huanglou Township Secondary School in the past month. I called an emergency meeting of the faculty this morning and it was decided that in order to conserve the students' physical strength and avoid recurrence of such unfortunate incidents, morning exercise and physical education classes will forthwith be suspended. All weekly physical labor classes are also suspended. During the time freed up by the suspended classes, students will study by themselves in their classrooms."

The principal's decision was met with murmuring among the girls but caused an outcry among the boys. Liu Tingsong protested loudly, "What's the fun in coming to school if we don't get physical education? I can't accept it!"

He was severely upbraided by Teacher Jin, "Liu Tingsong! That was inappropriate!"

While the way Liu Tingsong put it might not be the most tactful, Ma Xiaolong thought: He did have a point there. If a school does away with physical education, what would become of it? It would be such a dead place. Although small in build, Ma Xiaolong loved sports. He was second to none of his classmates in high jump and track sports. In table tennis he was the champion of the entire school. Still, he supported the decision announced by the principal. It had been quite a hardship coping with the demands of the physical education classes of late. That ladleful of porridge he had eaten at breakfast did not last even to the first class of the day; there was no energy left when it was time to run and jump in the sports field. It was not uncommon for him to be so famished when they assembled on the field for the physical education class, that his legs started to shake and he wanted to lie down on the grass and pass out; sometimes he'd see stars when he stopped after a run. After all, they had nothing in their stomach, and hadn't had a proper, filling meal in months. How could they be expected to be steady on their feet under this circumstance? Even when they were studying in the classroom, let alone when they had to jump and run on the sport field, their contracting, empty guts gave them painful cramps. The phys-ed and physical labor classes simply couldn't go on as usual.

Principal Pockmark tapped on the microphone and asked for silence. He went on, "The second matter I'd like to raise is the theft of some of the day students' lunch boxes from the steamer in the kitchen. This has gone on for several days now. Yesterday three day students had their lunch boxes stolen. Imagine stealing someone else's lunch box and causing that person to go hungry! What kind of behavior is that? Those three students came to me in tears yesterday and I had to use my own meal tickets to buy lunches for them so that they didn't have to go hungry. Like you all, I don't get enough to eat and I have no meal tickets to spare to help those students out."

A hush came over the student body. The silence was broken only by the frightened calls of two sparrows flying overhead.

Principal Pockmark continued, "Everyone is hungry, but that's no reason to lose one's moral bearings or stoop to baseness. I am giving notice that we have some preliminary clues about the thefts and I await the surrender of the perpetrator in my office. If the student who stole the lunch boxes comes to me today or tomorrow to confess to the thefts, I am ready to forgive that person and forgo all punishment. If, however, the perpetrator still tries to muddle through past the two-day deadline, I, as principal, will show no leniency."

A ripple of whispering passed among the audience; meanwhile Principal Pockmark waved a hand and barked from the dais, "Dismissed!"

Ma Xiaolong realized that for some reason the principal's gloomy stare was fixed on Class 6 of Ninth Grade, or more ominously, maybe even on Ma Xiaolong himself. What could this mean? He wondered.

He was roused from his reverie by Teacher Jin, who came up to him and whispered, "Ma Xiaolong, you can skip the first class. The principal wants to have a word with you in his office."

These words, although whispered, were still overheard by some, and many pairs of eyes turned as one to look on the face of Ma Xiaolong, who became flustered, as if he were a criminal who'd just been nabbed.

Liu Tingsong enjoyed a moment of schaden-freude, crying, "Ma Xiaolong, you've been called to the principal's office! So you must be the thief who stole the day students' lunch boxes."

Ma Xiaolong's face flushed furiously; he shot a fierce look at Liu Tingsong and was on the point of giving a sharp reply but checked himself. After dismissal, the students made their way back to class but he fell back, alone.

The first class of the day was class teacher Mr. Jin's reading. Teacher Jin was not his usual energetic, eloquent self this morning, but appeared weary and somewhat distracted. His eyes kept going back wistfully to the two vacant seats.

One of the seats had previously been occupied by Fan Yuling and the other was Ma Xiaolong's place. On Fan Yuling's desk, her stationery case and homework book lay unopened. Someone had picked a wild flower growing on school grounds and placed the grayish white flower, very conspicuously, on top of the stationery case. Teacher Jin seemed afraid to look at the empty seat or the wild flower, but time and again his eyes were drawn involuntarily back to the spot.

Finally his eyes rested on the wild flower, un-moving, and red around the rims.

He broke his silence and said, "I did not do a good job of protecting Fan Yuling. I am responsible for her fainting on the sports field ..."

Teacher Jin covered his face with his book and his shoulders started heaving. The students had never seen a male teacher sob before and the sight was a shock to them. The girls all started crying with him and the boys bowed their heads.

The classroom now reverberated with the sound of weeping. After a short while Luo Zhaoying rose to her feet and said, "Teacher Jin, I saw something Fan Yuling did but I don't know if I am allowed to speak about it."

Teacher Jin looked at her with his tear-misted eyes and said, "Please do."

Luo Zhaoying said, "In the past few days I often saw Fan Yuling leave the table with her bowl of food during meal times. It struck me as very odd. Day before yesterday when she left the table during breakfast, and again during lunch, I couldn't help following her ..."

Teacher Jin asked, "Where did she go?"

Luo Zhaoying said, "She took her bowl to the school entrance. I saw a boy about seven or eight years old, waiting barefoot by the gate ..."

A student at the back of the class said, "Fan Yuling had a younger brother. It was her younger brother."

Luo Zhaoying said, "I guessed as much. Fan Yuling gave her bowl of food to him and he wolfed it down. Before leaving, he said he'd come back in the evening ..."

Teacher Jin said, with sudden understanding, "So, that means Fan Yuling forwent several meals, and gave her own food to her younger brother instead!"

Luo Zhaoying said, "She did the same for lunch day before yesterday. I saw it."

Teacher Jin walked in silence to Fan Yuling's desk, picked up the wild flower and looked at it as tears ran down his cheeks.

A hush came over the class. The air was so heavy it was hard to breathe. All eyes were now focused on that empty chair; everyone was remembering the way she hunched over the desk when she wrote, and her laughter …

It was sometime before the class started, as it were, to breathe again. Teacher Jin picked up his book, closed his eyes in an effort to regain his composure, and asked the class to read with him:

"But during mild and bright spring weather, then the waves are unruffled and the azure translucence above and below stretches before your eyes for myriads of *li*, when the water-birds fly down to congregate on the sands and fish with scales like glimmering silk disport themselves in the water, when the iris and orchids on the banks grow luxuriant and green; or when dusk falls over this vast expanse and bright moon casts its light a thousand *li*, when the rolling waves glitter like gold and silent shadows in the water glimmer like jade, and the fishermen sing to each other for sheer joy." (*Yueyang Pavilion* written by Fan Zhongyan [989–1052], translation by Gladys Yang and Yang Xianyi)

What an exquisite description of spring was given in this delectable piece of ancient Chinese literature! But the recitation by the class was anemic, lackadaisical and depressed in tone.

It was then that the door was nudged open gently and Ma Xiaolong appeared in the doorway, with a vacant look in his eyes. The class's attention now moved from their books to his face.

Teacher Jin said, "Go back to your seat."

Ma Xiaolong sat down in his chair, but his mind was somewhere else. His eyes fell sometimes unseeingly on the blackboard and sometimes ostensibly on his book, the Chinese characters in it becoming increasingly unreal for him. The teacher's words flew out of the classroom and hung in the air, sounding like echoes in a mountain valley.

Since starting his attendance at Huanglou Township Secondary School, Ma Xiaolong had never been so distracted and uneasy.

Luo Zhaoying tried all morning to find a chance to speak to Ma Xiaolong but he sat with his head bowed all that time; besides, with all eyes on him, she found it hard to have a private word with him. But Liu Tingsong, determined not to leave Ma Xiaolong alone, provocatively tapped him on his shoulder and asked, "Why did the principal want to speak to you? Was it about the theft of the day students' lunch boxes?"

Glum-faced, Ma Xiaolong studiously ignored him, but it was plain that deep down he felt a towering rage. When he occasionally threw a glance up, his eyes would shoot forth an arc of sparks.

At lunch time the refectory was, as usual, abuzz with voices.

The fare was growing worse: Everyone got a mixed-grain steamed bun, plus a ladleful of vegetable soup. The mixed-grain bun was dark like a caked lump of clay; the vegetable soup was so clear you could see the bottom, with a few pieces of vegetable leaves floating limply on the surface and not a speck of fat detectable.

From the eight enamel bowls of various sizes arranged on the table, Luo Zhaoying, the head of table, first took Fan Yuling's two bowls, filled one with a ladleful of soup and placed a black bun in the other.

Ma Xiaolong and Liu Tingsong watched in silence as Luo Zhaoying finished filling Fan Yuling's bowls and placed them carefully in a corner of the table, where Fan Yuling used to sit. Luo Zhaoying froze for a moment, and silent tears rolled down her cheeks as she looked at the two familiar bowls.

A lump rose in Ma Xiaolong's throat; his eyes too began to moisten. Afraid that he might be unable to restrain his sobbing, he picked up his bun and soup and hurried out of the refectory to squat down against the exterior wall and ate his lunch there.

Liu Tingsong quickly wolfed down his portion and brought Fan Yuling's lunch over to his place. Before Luo Zhaoying had a chance to make an observation, Liu Tingsong had already taken a big bite out of the black bun. He then slurped up a mouthful of soup, with which he noisily washed down the bite of bun. Raising his eyes to fix a stare on Luo Zhaoying, he said, "What are you staring at me for? She is dead. Are you telling me we should let her portion go to waste?"

Luo Zhaoying, her eyes red-rimmed, pressed her lips together a number of times, without forming her thoughts into words. She quickly finished her lunch and made her way, with clenched teeth, to the office in charge of meals at the back of the refectory, where she had Fan Yuling removed from the list of meal subscriptions and received a refund of 6.50 yuan from the teacher on duty. She carefully wrapped the money in her handkerchief and put it in an inside pocket of her quilted jacket.

Shortly after that, she set off toward the town post office, where she and Ma Xiaolong had agreed to meet. Standing outside the post office, she kept looking in the direction of the school but there was no sign of Ma Xiaolong. She wondered if Ma Xiaolong could have stood her up. Now that Fan Yuling was dead, he might decide the agreement made this morning no longer stood.

Standing there, Luo Zhaoying felt nervous, as students from her school walked past her with curious or startled glances in her direction. There were both day students and boarders, with familiar faces, though no one in her own class. She was apprehensive about being found out meeting with Ma Xiaolong here. If they were seen together gossip would race around the school like a wild fire.

It was not until about half past twelve that

Ma Xiaolong arrived in a hurry. Luo Zhaoying immediately dragged him into a narrow alley and complained, "What's the matter? I almost thought you were not coming."

Ma Xiaolong said, "How could I not come? We had an agreement!"

Luo Zhaoying asked, "Why did you take so long then?"

Ma Xiaolong explained, "I couldn't find my fruit candies. I had put them under my pillow but they were gone."

Luo Zhaoying held Ma Xiaolong's eyes and said, "Could he have taken them?" They understood that "he" always meant Liu Tingsong.

Ma Xiaolong said, "Who knows? I didn't catch him in the act, so I can't pin it on him without proof."

Luo Zhaoying answered, "What's gone is gone. At least I still have my biscuits."

Ma Xiaolong added, "I bought five peanut candies at a store on my way here. Fan Yuling liked peanut candies."

The two took a shortcut to the clinic. Luo Zhaoying knew a nurse she called San Yi, or "auntie," at the outpatient section of the clinic, who was from the same hamlet. Luo Zhaoying asked her, "My classmate Fan Yuling died here. Has her family taken her home?"

San Yi said, "Rotten luck! Her mother died when she was little and her father is a traveling carpenter working out of town. So we haven't been able to contact her family yet. Only her little brother came to the clinic, but he's too young to know what to do, so we can't rely on him."

Ma Xiaolong asked, "Where is Fan Yuling now?"

San Yi said, "She's lying in the morgue. Oh rotten luck!"

After a while, San Yi asked, "Do you mean you want to see her?"

Ma Xiaolong nodded, "Yes, we do."

San Yi assured him, "That's not a problem, I have the keys. It's only right that you should pay last respects to her. You were classmates after all. Follow me."

With that, San Yi led the two teenagers out of the main building and brought them to the northwest corner. From a distance they could make out the three Chinese characters of morgue on a wooden plaque above a door. Luo Zhaoying stopped in her tracks and said, "San Yi ..."

San Yi turned her head round, "What is it?"

Luo Zhaoying mumbled, "I am nervous. I don't think I'll go in."

San Yi said with a dismissive curl of her mouth, "What's gotten into you?"

Ma Xiaolong said, "There's nothing to be afraid of. I'm not scared."

San Yi said, "So what's it going to be? Make up your minds. I've to go back to my duties."

Luo Zhaoying replied, "San Yi, you go back to work! We will not go in to see her."

San Yi grumbled as she turned round and left.

Ma Xiaolong said to Luo Zhaoying, "I can't get over how easily frightened you are! What's there to be afraid of? She was your classmate! Didn't we come here in order to see her one last time?"

Luo Zhaoying's eyes crisscrossed the ground in nervous silence. Ma Xiaolong cast a sidelong glance at her and found her face had turned ashen. He figured the pallor must be from fear, so he stopped grumbling.

Snatches of the refrains of the song *Let's Pull the Oars* sung by a children's choir drifted into earshot; it was the broadcast of West Town Elementary School. When he heard the tune, Ma Xiaolong seemed to sense the gentle landing of something from a great distance, and his chest was flooded with such a warm feeling that it almost hurt. He had graduated from West Town Elementary School, where he spent six years of his life. Elementary school was not that long ago, but it seemed to have drifted so far from him.

They stopped as they approached the door to the morgue.

It was a wide, double door. There was a ramp leading up to it, obviously for the use of push carts and gurneys. Luo Zhaoying took a handkerchief out of a pocket, spread it on the ramp near the door and put some biscuits on the handkerchief.

Facing the door with a dispirited look, Luo Zhaoying said softly, "Fan Yuling, Ma Xiaolong and I are here to see you. I don't have strong nerves ... so I'll just talk to you from out here."

Ma Xiaolong squatted on his heels and took the five peanut candies out of pocket and arranged them carefully at the side of the biscuits.

A draft of air, very cold and very hard, blew out through the gap between the double door and the top of the ramp, swirling and swooshing between Ma Xiaolong's fingers. Wrinkling his nose to sniff the air, he detected a smell of medicated soap. That must be the odor surrounding Fan Yuling, he thought, and she must lie just behind the double door. Would her face be covered by a white sheet? In movies, when someone died in a hospital, a nurse would pull up a white sheet to cover the face.

Luo Zhaoying ferreted out a piece of paper from a pocket and set it on the ground; it was a history quiz. A gust of wind flipped the sheet over, and Ma Xiaolong hastened to find a small pebble with which to weigh it down. When he was doing this, he glimpsed, at the upper right corner, the score of 83 out of a hundred, marked in red by the teacher.

Luo Zhaoying said, "Fan Yuling, your history quiz was marked. You got 83. Teacher Liu had nothing but praise for you, saying you'd made good progress and achieved balanced performance across the subjects."

Ma Xiaolong nodded quietly, as if the three were chatting at the refectory table.

Luo Zhaoying went on and said, "Fan Yuling, you had been worried these past few days that if you did not do well in history, there would be talk that you excelled in math only and did poorly in the rest of the disciplines. Now you don't need to worry anymore …"

Ma Xiaolong chimed in, "Fan Yuling, this should set your mind at ease."

Luo Zhaoying continued, "Fan Yuling, I already canceled your meal subscriptions and there was a refund of 6.5 yuan, which I handed over to Teacher Jin. He said he would hand it to your father when he comes to the school."

At this time a boy with a dirty appearance put his head around the corner of the building and Luo Zhaoying instantly recognized him. She asked, "You must be Fan Yuling's little brother."

The boy nodded.

Ma Xiaolong gestured with his hand, saying, "Come here."

After a brief hesitation, the boy emerged from behind the wall. He walked timidly up to the two middle school students. After a while he gestured toward the door of the morgue and said to the students, "My older sister lying in there."

Luo Zhaoying and Ma Xiaolong exchanged a look.

In the meantime the boy's eyes were drawn to the biscuits and candies on the ground. He crouched down and touched the biscuits lightly with his index finger before looking up at the two students.

Ma Xiaolong and Luo Zhaoying exchanged another look.

The boy nudged the biscuits again with his

finger, and, seeing that the two students didn't raise any objection, grabbed one biscuit and stuffed it into his mouth. As he chewed, he fixed his eyes nervously on the two students.

Ma Xiaolong had a hand out and was on the point of saying something when Luo Zhaoying checked him.

Luo Zhaoying said to the boy, "We are going back to class. Take your time. Don't choke on them."

The rims of her eyes reddened as she said it. After taking a few steps, she turned her head around and said, "When you see your father, tell him to come to the school as soon as possible. Our teacher wants to speak to him. All right?"

The boy, his mouth crammed full with biscuits, assented with his head, his eyes shining.

After leaving the clinic they picked deserted alleys as they made their way back to the school. When they were some distance from town, Luo Zhaoying asked Ma Xiaolong, "What did the principal call you into his office for, this morning?"

Ma Xiaolong kept walking, with his head bowed and did not utter a word.

Luo Zhaoying raised her voice, saying, "Hey, I was asking you a question."

It was only then that Ma Xiaolong lifted his head and said, with a glance at Luo Zhaoying, "I don't feel like talking about it."

Luo Zhaoying shot a baleful look at him, saying, "So you don't feel like talking about it. For your information I am not interested in hearing about it."

With the school gate looming in sight, the two, as if by previous agreement, put a distance between themselves. Luo Zhaoying quickened her pace to walk ahead of him and went into the gate with a nimble twist of her slender waist. Ma Xiaolong, on the other hand, slowed down to fall back and ambled deliberately to the other side of the road, dragging out the time of his reentry into the school.

2

This was the third time Ma Xiaolong was summoned to the principal's office. The first time his father Ma Changsong, who had been an accountant at the school for a long time, took him there. To be precise, he had worked there since the school came into existence. One might almost say Huanglou Township Secondary School was built to the clicking sound of his abacus. One would have expected him to have been elevated to a higher post, such as Chief of General Services, given his unparalleled seniority, but year after year he sat in the same corner of the Office of General Services, working away on his abacus, at the beck and call of a much younger low-level cadre transferred to the school from the town government. Ma Xiaolong knew all this was attributable to his father's former service as a military doctor in the Kuomintang army.

When his father brought him into the principal's office, his father said to Principal Pockmark, "He is my third child; he just passed the admission test."

Principal Pockmark looked up first at Ma Xiaolong, then at the accountant and said, "Just passed the admission test, did he? Very well! Which class has he been assigned to?"

Ma Xiaolong didn't understand why it was that every time his father entered the principal's office, his voice would start to tremble and the stoop in his shoulders would be more pronounced than usual.

His father replied, "Class 6 of Seventh Grade, I think. Teacher Jin Hexiang's class."

Principal Pockmark said, "Good. Teacher Jin is a nice person."

Ma Changsong nodded emphatically, "Yes, yes indeed."

He had his second rendezvous in the principal's office accompanied by his aunt Zheng Xiuli. The Education Department of the county had just issued a new rule stipulating that every middle school had to be equipped with a doctor's office and Principal Pockmark got frustrated after a hectic few days of searching for a doctor to take the position. He came to Ma Xiaolong's father and said, "I understand that your sister-in-law is a doctor in the clinic. Can you do me a favor and try to persuade her to become our school doctor?" At the principal's suggestion, Ma Changsong went to lobby Zheng Xiuli but was met the same day with a flat refusal. Zheng Xiuli said, "I am doing fine at the clinic; why would I want to quit and work for a cash-strapped school?" Ma Changsong tried several more times and even mobilized the support of Ma Xiaolong's uncle, who had a job in another town, before Zheng Xiuli finally gave in. It was Ma Xiaolong who took her to see the principal in his office the day she reported for work. He brought his aunt to the principal, said this is my aunt, bowed and left the room. He did not know what the principal said to his aunt.

The third time he went into the principal's office—that was today—he was faced with a grim situation. The moment he walked in, the principal asked, "Do you know your father is in big trouble now?"

Ma Xiaolong's face blanched in terror. He remembered that when he went home the week before, his father was smoking and complaining, "Principal Pockmark got an advance of 2,000 yuan from the school account and he is now denying everything." His mother had asked, "Isn't there an IOU for the advance? How can he deny taking out an advance?" His father had answered, "Principal Pockmark told me it was for an emergency and he'd repay it shortly. So there was no IOU." His mother had said, "How could you have let him have such a large sum of money without an IOU? Was there any witness?" His father had answered, "That's the problem. There was nobody there to witness the transaction. I did enter it in the books, but the principal adamantly denies it, this is killing me ..."

Ma Xiaolong cast a timid glance at Principal Pockmark and said, "I didn't know."

Principal Pockmark said, "Is your family suddenly flush with cash? Have your father and mother bought you a lot of stuff?"

Ma Xiaolong said, "No, no, they haven't."

The principal said, "Your father embezzled a huge sum recently. You must persuade your father to come clean about it."

Ma Xiaolong said, "My father is not someone who would embezzle."

The principal said, "You are too young to understand. It was a large sum that Ma Changsong embezzled. If he does not come clean, then he will go to jail. What with his unsavory past, he will face a long jail time."

Ma Xiaolong suddenly felt dizzy and his knees gave, almost causing him kneel down in front of the principal.

It was late afternoon and the light in the corridor was already fading.

Ma Xiaolong walked slowly and listlessly along the wall, the index finger of his right hand scraping against the wall, making a scarcely audible rubbing sound. His thin silhouette was framed against the light at the end of the corridor, which echoed with his lonely footsteps.

Ma Xiaolong was making his way toward the

school doctor's office. He wanted to talk to his aunt Zheng Xiuli, and tell her what happened in the principal's office that day.

The door to the school doctor's office was open, but his aunt was not in the office. She probably went to the refectory to fetch her meal, he thought, and went in to sit by the window. He picked up a book lying on the desk. It was entitled, *Human Anatomy*. Ma Xiaolong immediately sneaked to the door in the wall that separated the sick bay from the outer office and looked out. There was no sign yet of his aunt, so he opened the book with trembling hands.

A few days before, when he was in this office, he had already taken a peek at this book. He had been profoundly struck by the drawings of the male and female reproductive organs in the book. When he had seen those color drawings for the first time, he felt his heart suddenly stop and he had difficulty breathing. It was only after a while that his blood resumed its tidal surge, which caused his head to throb violently. He had run his eyes greedily and hurriedly over those pictures, every pore of his skin dilating ...

He now turned the pages to that chapter again. He did not want to look at the pages about the male organs, which made him feel queasy. He had these organs too, but they were simple, clean and smooth. How come the book depicted them in such an ungainly light? He quickly flipped the pages to the female section. He was interested only in the female organs, which to him represented a deep labyrinth, whose convoluted twists and turns had a special aura and charm that called to him and tempted him. He looked at the pictures and the text in a state of excitement and tension, as burning hot blood churned deep inside his body. He had a strong urge to tuck the book in his clothes and smuggle it into his dorm so that he could study it more closely. But he did not have the audacity ...

He heard footsteps outside the door. Ma Xiaolong immediately put the copy of *Human Anatomy* back on the table. The footsteps stopped, but the voice was not his aunt's, but that of a man.

"Doctor Zheng! Doctor Zheng!"

The voice was low but urgent. Ma Xiaolong pricked up his ears and immediately recognized the voice of Principal Pockmark.

His aunt followed shortly and seemed to be in a hurry. The moment she entered the doctor's office, she opened the tap and washed her hands noisily.

Principal Pockmark grumbled in a low voice,

"Where have you been? I was looking for you everywhere!"

His aunt said, "I had to attend to a student in the dorm. It was a serious case of edema in both legs. The skin wouldn't spring back when I depressed it with a finger."

The principal asked, "Which class is the patient in?"

His aunt said, "Class 2 of Ninth Grade."

The principal asked again, "A boy or girl?"

His aunt said, "A boy."

The principal said, "What's the diagnosis?"

His aunt said, "Hunger! What else? His family couldn't make ends meet and did not produce enough of a rice crop to exchange for meal tickets at the school. All they gave him was a bag of bran. The boy ate this stuff in the dorm when nobody was around. It is no food for humans. You get constipation when you eat that kind of stuff. He's been eating it for five days and has not been able to have a bowel movement. His belly is distended like that of a mantis. I had to dig out the excrement with my finger. It was hard as rock!"

The principal said, "You are so nice to the students."

His aunt said, "I'm a school doctor. That's what

I do."

The principal said, "You don't have enough to eat yourself. You mustn't overwork."

His aunt said, "I'm already luckier than those kids."

The principal said, "I thought you might be hungry, so I've brought you some soybeans and peanuts. They are roasted and ready to eat."

At the mention of soybeans and peanuts, a quiver ran through Ma Xiaolong, who suddenly felt energized. It had been six months since he last tasted soybeans, a handful of them, brought back by Luo Zhaoying when she returned to school from her autumn home leave. That simply divine taste had been seared into his brain, and when he smacked his mouth he was sure he could still detect a residual soybean flavor in the gaps of his teeth. He could clearly remember a strange feeling he had on that memorable day, that after eating that handful of soybeans, even his flatulence had a pleasant smell! As for peanuts, he couldn't remember how long ago he had last tasted them. It was such a long time ago that he had forgotten what they looked like and what their color was, to say nothing of what they smelled like. The words of Principal Pockmark jolted him out of his lethargy.

He dashed to the door of the partition and lifted the curtain covering its glass sash to peek at the soybeans and peanuts brought by the Principal. He knew that as an official receiving a civilian commission upon his discharge from the army, he enjoyed a monthly alimentary bonus, including peanuts and soybeans. He saw two cloth sacks, each the size of a fist. He thought to himself: You are really cheap, Principal Pockmark! Is that all you are bringing my aunt? You should have brought more, so that my aunt could spare a handful for me too. I really crave the roasted peanuts and soybeans! To smell their aroma!

But despite the small size of the gift, Ma Xiaolong was really quite impressed by this feat by Principal Pockmark. He knew the Principal had given snacks to his aunt—it would be a small packet of peanuts, or half a sack of small dates, or a few sticks of fried dough twists. His aunt would not eat any of these cherished food items but would save them up for her Sunday home visit to offer the treats to her kids. Naturally she would give some to her nephew Ma Xiaolong. In those difficult times, few were the students in a town school like theirs who had a chance to taste treats such as fried dough twists and dates, soy beans or peanuts. For this reason Ma Xiaolong considered himself fortunate to have an aunt who treated him so decently. But at the same time he could not quite understand why Principal Pockmark, who had his own family and children to take care of, was giving so many treats to his aunt.

He saw his aunt pull out a drawer and stuff the two packets into it. Then she turned round, her face flushing and her eyes fixed on Principal Pockmark, to say, "If your wife were to find out, I wouldn't be surprised if she were to eat me up."

Principal Pockmark said with a chuckle, "I'm going to eat you up this moment …"

Principal Pockmark's hands reached into the front of his aunt's blouse from beneath the hem and went up to get hold of her two breasts and started to knead them. His aunt seemed quickly to curl up under the kneading hands, making moaning sounds and behaving as if she were ready to collapse. Principal Pockmark was murmuring something as his whole body went into frenzied movement; he glued his lips to hers and his hands, after busying themselves with her breasts, moved down to grope in the area of her waist. Ma Xiaolong saw his aunt squirm, as if to wriggle free from the roving hands, but at the same time she compliantly turned up her face to allow

Principal Pockmark to engage her mouth. He could hear the sound of the two mouths smacking together, a sound that reminded him of fish nibbling on algae.

Ma Xiaolong's eyes felt warm and bloated. He wanted to rub them but was afraid he would make a noise doing it. He wanted to close them for an instant, but was afraid to miss any part of the theater. His heart beat wildly and his chest was hot like a burning stove. The hot air issuing from his mouth was like the flames leaping out of a stove. He said in his mind: Ma Xiaolong, you shouldn't be looking at this. Stop looking! But his eyes, not blinking for a second, were glued to the two adults welded together on the other side of the glass sash.

Suddenly he heard a big bang out there. Ma Xiaolong winced. He saw the aluminum tray his aunt used to boil her syringes had tumbled off the table and fallen to the floor, scattering the syringes and needles far and wide and spilling the water.

But Principal Pockmark and his aunt were still tightly intertwined, oblivious to the racket. Ma Xiaolong saw his aunt's pants drop to the floor, like the furled sail of a small boat. Then it was the principal's pants' turn to drop to the floor, like the furled sail of a big boat.

It was all Ma Xiaolong could do to suppress his cry. He was seeing something like this for the first time ever in his life. A man and a woman stripped to their bare, pale skin and glued together like that felt surreal to him. He felt squeamish about continuing his voyeurism yet reluctant to take his eyes off the show.

He heard rustling sounds coming from the outer room, punctuated by his aunt's moans and the principal's bellows, which revolted Ma Xiaolong, because they sounded like a pig's grunting.

After a while, Principal Pockmark suddenly flung back his head and belted out two prolonged howls, and the two bodies finally separated. Ma Xiaolong saw his aunt's body in all its nakedness. It was the first time he had seen a woman's body so clearly. The felt an involuntary tensing and a hot wave surged across his groin ...

All through the evening self-study hours, Ma Xiaolong was in a distracted state. When he looked at his homework, all he saw were those two pale, naked bodies tightly locked together, moaning, pumping, quivering ... his heart beat wildly and the palms of his hands became clammy. Half-way through the study time, he still hadn't finished solving even one problem.

He dropped his head on the desk and closed his eyes.

His mouth felt parched and thirsty and his skin was burning; he was vexed and restless.

What the principal said to him that morning came back to him. He was worried about what would happen to his father, who already had the curse of historical baggage, and if he were charged with embezzlement, as Principal Pockmark seemed to suggest, it would be disastrous for his family. Needless to say, going on to high school would be out of the question for him as part of the fallout. What school would recruit the son of an embezzler? And if he couldn't get into high school, where would he, a middle school graduate, find a job? But Ma Xiaolong was convinced his father was not an embezzler. His father had always been a timid person fearful of getting into any kind of trouble. He was deferential to people and exhorted members of his household to the cultivation of forbearance and a conciliatory demeanor. He also cautioned them against the slightest breach of law or regulation. How could a person like that be capable of the kind of brazen,

audacious misdeed imputed to him? Was Principal
Pockmark trying to wriggle out of the repayment of
the advance he took against the school account by
accusing his father of embezzling those funds?

But that didn't sound logical to Ma Xiaolong:
How could Principal Pockmark stoop to such baseness? It was beyond his imagination that a middle
school principal, or for that matter a discharged
military officer turned civilian official, would do
something like framing an innocent old accountant
who had given many years of service to the school.

These questions threatened to overwhelm the
adolescent brain of Ma Xiaolong and the search for
answers was simply beyond him. He had thought
he would come to his aunt with these questions and
receive some ideas and advice from her. He was totally
unprepared for the shocking scene he happened onto
in the school doctor's office.

He was unsure if it boded well or ill. According
to the older folk, hearing a cat meowing in heat or
seeing two dogs in copulation brought bad luck.
If dogs and cats doing the stuff had such baleful
influence, what disaster would not rain on his head
from his witnessing humans—and an aunt and the
principal of his school too—engaged in the act?

He heard someone's voice: Ma Xiaolong, Teacher Zheng wants to see you.

Ma Xiaolong lifted his head to find his aunt Zheng Xiuli in her white coat in the doorway of the classroom waving at him with a smile on her face. The evening self-study class was becoming so boring that the slightest disturbance was a welcome distraction and the forty odd pairs of eyes instantly swung, in military uniformity and precision, toward the woman doctor in the doorway and a buzz of discussion sprang up. Ma Xiaolong found his aunt prettier than usual this evening, her eyes dancing and bright and her lips red and glossy as if she had applied lipstick. Even her white coat appeared smarter than usual. But he felt somewhat embarrassed to have her wave at him before the roomful of classmates.

He got to his feet and crossed to the door, with all eyes boring into his back.

His aunt reached out a long arm to grab him before he even reached the doorway and turned around and walked Ma Xiaolong a few paces away from the roomful of eyes. She said, "I can see that Xiaolong is feeling bashful because Auntie has come to his class to see him." Ma Xiaolong looked at the floor without speaking.

His aunt said, "There's no reason to feel awkward. I am your aunt after all. You should feel lucky that you have an aunt to look in on you. Ask the other kids in the class if they have the same kind of luck."

She chuckled as she said it.

Ma Xiaolong thought to himself: You can laugh, but I want to weep. Do you realize that Principal Pockmark is forcing Father to confess to the embezzlement of two thousand yuan? Do you know Father has been fretting about this at home?

Ma Xiaolong turned his back on her spitefully. Zheng Xiuli tugged at his hand to make him turn round and said in a low voice, "Auntie has some goodies for you today. Guess what they are?"

Ma Xiaolong kept silent, his head bowed and a look of revulsion in his averted eyes.

Like a prestidigitator, Zheng Xiuli whipped out, from a pocket of her white coat, a small cloth sack, and held it out under Ma Xiaolong's nose, "Smell it! Guess what it is!"

Ma Xiaolong stiffened his neck and moved his nose aside. He knew what his aunt held in her hand. He saw Principal Pockmark place it on the table in the school doctor's office. He had also seen the principal and his aunt drop their pants to the floor and strip down to their bare skin. When they had done that, the two small cloth sacks sat not far from them.

It was then that Ma Xiaolong's nostrils were assailed by an odious, shameful odor. He had no idea how this odor materialized at this moment.

His aunt said, "These are roasted peanuts! It must have been years since you last tasted them."

And his aunt pressed the small sack into Ma Xiaolong's hand.

Ma Xiaolong involuntarily flinched and drew back, as if he had touched a live wire, and flung the bag of peanuts violently onto the corridor floor. As he turned and walked away, he shouted, "I don't want them! I don't want them!"

His aunt Zheng Xiuli was dumbfounded. Her face went pale as she looked at the boy's angry back. She had always known Ma Xiaolong as a gentle, well-behaved boy. This nephew's exemplary academic achievement in school had done her proud among her colleagues. She had often brought him treats and no matter the size or the flavor he had always accepted them cheerfully. He was after all a boy who was still growing and was always half starved. Why did he react the way he did today?

Zheng Xiuli's emotion was one of resentment

and sadness. She was clueless about the reason for his aberrant behavior.

Ma Xiaolong went back grim-faced to the classroom. He could sense without looking that the entire class was following him with their eyes. Ignoring them, he plumped down in his chair. After a while, he picked up his pen to start on his homework but soon threw it down in disgust and dropped his head on his arms.

He saw nothing but darkness and he could smell the odor of his own breath, which was warm and mixed with the scent of wood and dust. This warmth and darkness afforded him some quiet and sense of security.

But peace of mind eluded him. He was himself perplexed by his freshness toward his aunt just now. He had never had an attitude problem before, not to anyone, let alone to his own aunt, who was unfailingly kind to him, causing some classmates to mistake her for his mother.

With his head still cradled in his arms on his desk, Ma Xiaolong felt a sudden dizziness and a burning sensation in his nostrils. He wiped his nose reflexively and found the back of his hand covered with warm blood.

His nose was bleeding! Ma Xiaolong's heart sank, as if into a cold pit.

Just then Luo Zhaoying passed his desk and surreptitiously touched his arm; she left a note on the desk.

Startled, Ma Xiaolong quickly snatched up the note and stuffed it into a pocket. Then he fished out some sheets of crude toilet paper from his book bag and stopped his nostrils with them. He knew he was supposed to tilt his head back to stop the nosebleed faster, but he was afraid that if he did so, Liu Tingsong and his cohorts would be on to the fact that he had a nosebleed and would have their moment of schadenfreude. They would surely whoop with joy.

So he kept his head down to wait for the bleeding to stop. As he passed his tongue over the inside of his mouth, he detected the sweet and salty scent of blood travelling through the tip of his tongue to every corner of his body.

A long time passed but the bloody scent had not dissipated; Ma Xiaolong couldn't wait any longer. The thought of Luo Zhaoying's note quickened his heartbeat once again. He surveyed his surrounding out of the corner of his eyes and having made sure no one was looking he got the note out and stole a quick glance at the line of written words in a small hand: Some people are planning to hurt you this evening. Watch out!

Ma Xiaolong heard a roar in his head, as if it had just suffered a blow. He was only 15, and had no idea what "hurt" signified or how serious it was and what the consequences would be. But he vaguely sensed that there must be a plot and a few shady co-conspirators behind the word "hurt." He could not clearly picture those faces but he could hear their laughter ...

He rose to his feet once again and went out the door to catch up with Luo Zhaoying. He pulled her to a dark corner and asked anxiously, "How did you find out there were people who planned on hurting me?"

Luo Zhaoying said, "When I was in the lavatory I overheard some guys talking in the boys' stalls next door. They were saying they wanted to draw blood from you tonight just to show you what they are capable of ..."

Ma Xiaolong said, "Could you tell by listening who they were?"

Luo Zhaoying said, "There were some voices I don't recognize but at least I did hear Liu Tingsong's voice."

Ma Xiaolong said, "How were they going to hurt me?"

Luo Zhaoying said, "I wasn't able to make out the rest of their conversation."

Ma Xiaolong felt as if his heart was in a vise and he had difficulty breathing. He felt a black shroud had been wrapped tightly around him, to tie him down and to asphyxiate him. On the dark shroud several pairs of eyes floated about, smiling maliciously at him. Hands reached out, to close around his neck ...

Luo Zhaoying said, "Why don't you go home now. At least you'll be safe for tonight if you do that." Ma Xiaolong said, "Me, go home now? Home is dozens of kilometers away. How do you expect me to accomplish that?"

Luo Zhaoying said, "Or we can report it to the teacher on duty. What do you think?"

Ma Xiaolong said, "How do we do that? Do we say you overheard a conversation in the boys' lavatory? You think you can bring yourself to say that?"

Luo Zhaoying whispered after a long silence, "I've got it! You go and sleep at your aunt's place tonight and you'll be safe."

Looking at Luo Zhaoying in the dark, Ma Xiaolong quietly shook his head.

Back in the classroom, Ma Xiaolong found he was more bothered than before. When he turned around to borrow a compass from the classmate sitting behind him, he stole a glance in the direction of Liu Tingsong only to meet his eyes as he happened to be looking in his direction. Ma Xiaolong immediately averted his eyes. He saw in Liu Tingsong's expression scheming and malice, and an indescribable menace. A cold shiver went down his spine.

Try as he might, he couldn't picture how Liu Tingsong and his acolytes were going to "draw blood." This was the first time he heard such a terrifying term, and yet it came out so easily from the lips of people like Liu Tingsong. Would they plunge a dagger into his chest? Or slit his throat with a knife? Why else would they use the term "draw blood"? Maybe he should, as a precaution, put a knife under his pillow, just in case ...

The nosebleed at study-hall the previous evening came once more to Ma Xiaolong's mind. The blood on the back of his hand was so red, so warm and so sticky. When Liu Tingsong talked to his buddies about "drawing blood," it had to mean much more copious than the amount of his nosebleed. He could possibly bleed to death. He just couldn't understand what Liu Tingsong and his gang held against him. He searched in vain in his memory for any major grudge between them. He couldn't think of even any minor run-ins with them.

For a long time that night Ma Xiaolong lay in bed wide awake with apprehension. He kept telling himself: Ma Xiaolong, you mustn't fall asleep! Don't close your eyes, for some people are watching you with malice in their eyes. The moment you doze off, they may quietly come up to you and slit your throat with a sharp knife ...

In the dim light Ma Xiaolong's eyes wandered from time to time in the direction of Liu Tingsong's bed. He had gone to bed before Ma Xiaolong and was snoring loudly, like a pig. The snoring reassured him a little, for he thought that as long as Liu Tingsong was asleep, the matter of "drawing blood" was not an immediate concern. But he couldn't totally let down his guard, for it was not to be excluded that Liu Tingsong might have bought off someone else to do the dirty work for him. And what if he had planned it for after he had fallen sleep?

Thus he willed his eyelids to stay open and watched from inside his mosquito netting. He also kept his ears pricked up for the slightest unusual sound inside and outside the dorm room. It was late autumn and only a few mosquitos buzzed patiently close to the net; one or two bats flew in and out through the window, circling a few times in the room before flying out again; rodents darted about excitedly on the floor and along beams; crickets chirped here and there, lackadaisically and disjointedly, failing to create a chorus ... He couldn't see or hear anything that appeared out of the ordinary.

He was so drowsy. Ma Xiaolong's face felt dry and rough and his eyelids drooped repeatedly despite his effort at staying awake. Whenever he was drifting off to sleep, he would wake with a start, and he would pinch his thigh hard to keep sleep at bay with self-inflicted pain. He cautioned himself: This is a life-or-death moment. You mustn't fall asleep. For if you do, you may never wake up again!

But he was only a child after all and was at an age when the body demands a great deal of food and sleep. Sleep overtook him well before midnight.

Nothing happened that night. All was quiet the following night, and the night following that.

He began to doubt the accuracy of the information scribbled on Luo Zhaoying's note. A few days later, Luo Zhaoying herself observed to him at the refectory table, "Maybe I heard wrong. Or what they were planning in the toilet was aimed at someone other than you?"

Ma Xiaolong's eyes were wide open but there was a vacant look in them.

3

Just as Ma Xiaolong had almost forgotten about the whole thing disaster struck.

That night, Ma Xiaolong had one dream after another. First he dreamed of a big bird carrying a bag of roasted peanuts in its beak, flapping its wings in mid-air, gliding in lazy spirals. For all his jumping into the air with up-stretched hands, the peanuts remained out of reach. Then he dreamed he went into a narrow alley in town. It was dark and long, and quiet like a tunnel. The moment he entered it, Ma Xiaolong was gripped by fear. His head bent, he accelerated his pace, hoping to emerge from it as quickly as possible. To his bewilderment, no matter how fast he walked, the narrow alley still stretched before him, dark and seemingly endless. He panicked; he could hear his own heart beating in the quiet of the alley. Suddenly a dark silhouette detached itself from the shadow of a doorway. It was a big dog. The animal glared at him with fierce-looking eyes and kept barking at him, making a loud racket like that of exploding firecrackers. Ma Xiaolong broke into a frantic run, with the big dog in hot pursuit, running faster and faster, its panting breath close behind him. Ma Xiaolong's heart beat in panic like a drum, but his feet appeared glued to the ground, making it impossible for him to run off. And the steaming, long tongue of the big dog was now only inches from his calves ...

Ma Xiaolong woke up with a scream. It was then that he saw a real dog, about half the height of an adult, staring at him through the opening of the mosquito net!

Ma Xiaolong let out a sharp cry and nearly passed out with fright. Before he realized what was happening the dog started barking loudly. He curled up into a ball and backed into a far corner of the bed, staring at the dog in terror. Like the dog in his dream, the beast also had a fierce look in its eyes and his barking was as loud as exploding firecrackers. Two policemen stood behind the big dog, one plump and the other lean in form. The lean one pulled tightly at the leash restraining the dog; the fat one fixed a cold stare at Ma Xiaolong.

This was the first time he ever got so close to a big dog or to policemen.

The fat policeman said, "Get dressed and get down from your bed!"

The big dog barked a few more times and quieted down only after the lean policeman patted it on the head and stroked it roughly. Ma Xiaolong hurried into his clothes but when he got down from the bed his shoes were nowhere to be found. In a fluster he walked barefoot past the big dog. He found Liu Tingsong, who slept across from him, already awake, sitting at one end of his bed, looking with alarm at the big dog and the police, his face a little pale. Ma Xiaolong suspected that this scene was new to Liu Tingsong too. Then Ma Xiaolong's attention was drawn to the crowd gathered near the doorway, including teachers and school fellows, both from Class 6 of Ninth Grade and other classes. He could only conclude, from the sensation it had created, that something of gravity had happened.

The fat policeman grabbed Ma Xiaolong's arm and had him stand against the wall. As the lean policeman loosened his grip on its leash, the dog let out a woof and, nimbly lowering its head and its long profile slipped under Ma Xiaolong's bed. A moment later, it backed out from under the bed, first carrying out one shoe, then another, in its mouth. Finally it emerged, panting, dragging out a big bag. The sack was made of cloth and of flimsy construction, and the canines of the dog tore a big hole in it, out of which cascaded pieces of gleaming white rice.

Ma Xiaolong was flabbergasted.

All the teachers and students looking on were struck dumb.

Seeing that the dog had stopped foraging, the lean policeman bent down and poked under the bed with the handle of a broom. Three aluminum lunch boxes came into view one by one, making a hollow metallic sound against the cement floor, which particularly grated on the ears of the onlookers in the otherwise quiet night.

With dropped jaw, Ma Xiaolong was rendered speechless. He was mystified by the discovery of these items under his bed and wondered when they had been stashed there. How did the police and the big dog know to look under his bed?

Clearly he had not yet become fully conscious of the gravity of the situation. He had not yet had time to grasp the significance of what was unfolding. But he was clearly conscious of one thing: with each new item that the dog ferreted out from under his bed, the fat policeman's grip further tightened on his arm, like a vise. He could sense the throbbing of panic in the veins of his arm clamped in that vise.

There had been a major incident at the school that day.

Early that morning when Fatso Xu, the breakfast cook, went into the rice storage room to get the rice for the morning meal, he discovered when he threw on the light switch that the rice store was a mess, with rice strewn all over the floor. When he looked up he saw a big hole had been dug through the wall, with brick fragments next to it and the weeds growing outside the wall was visible in the light of the electric bulb.

Fatso Xu went limp with fright and sank to the floor, wetting his pants. He waved his arms and stirred his legs, wanting to call for help, but there was a tight constriction in his throat that prevented him from forming a sound. Recovering his wits, Fatso Xu struggled up and staggered toward the dorm of the teacher on duty, where he said falteringly, "The rice store ... was robbed! Someone dug a hole in the wall ... and robbed the rice store!"

The teacher on duty that day happened to be Teacher Jin, the class teacher of Class 6 of Ninth Grade. The information threw Teacher Jin into a panic also. While he was the teacher on duty, he was specifically put in charge of staying the night to watch over the boarding students only; he had no authority to make any major decisions. He immediately telephoned Principal Pockmark to report the incident. The principal yelled at him on the phone, "What the hell are you calling me for? Report it right away to the police station in the town!"

By the time the principal arrived, the police had already preceded him to the school. Theft from a government food store being a felony, the town police station had reported it to the county public security apparatus. When the two forensic detectives dispatched to the school by the county police had surveyed the crime scene at Huanglou Township Secondary School, they phoned the county police headquarters to say that as the crime was relatively recent and the crime scene indicators and evidence were fresh and clear, they would send a sniffing dog down immediately.

The German shepherd, panting, with its red tongue sticking out of its mouth, was driven to the school in the back of a jeep. It was time for the boarding students to get up from bed, and when the fat policeman, who headed the county team, heard the wake-up bell, he looked at his watch and asked the principal, "What's the bell for?"

Principal Pockmark said, "It is the morning call for the boarding students."

The team leader asked, "How many boarders are there?"

Principal Pockmark said, "Over a hundred."

The fat policeman said in a distressed tone, "If the hundred students got out of bed at this time, all the evidence would be disturbed by them. Give the order to those students to stay in their beds. They will not get out of bed without my orders!"

Principal Pockmark shot a baleful glance at him, which meant: Quit acting important! You are but a county policeman. Do you have any idea who you are speaking so insolently to? When I was second in command of a regiment before I retired from the military, you were probably eating grass in some damn backwater hamlet!

But in view of the serious and urgent nature of the incident, he decided to let the matter slide. He summoned Teacher Jin and Fatso Xu and told them to make the rounds of the dorm rooms with a bullhorn to pass on the order.

Finding themselves for the first time in a situation like this, the students had been panicked and bewildered by the order shouted out of the bullhorns. They curled up in their beds, grumbling and cursing. Ma Xiaolong alone was out of character that day and was still fast asleep at this hour, oblivious to the mind-boggling theft.

That huge German shepherd, conducted by the lean county policeman, made a round first in the rice store, then went, with its heavy, panting breath, out of the student refectory. Sniffing the scents along the way, the big dog headed straight for the northeast corner of the campus, where it uncovered, by the fence wall, a makeshift stove with smoldering embers. After walking around a few times in the vicinity of the stove in the ground, the big dog continued its northeast rush. The lean policeman followed, with the dog loosely held on the leash. The big dog broke into a trot and led them straight to the dorm of Class 6 of Ninth Grade, to the bed of Ma Xiaolong, and nudged open the mosquito net. Having never before witnessed a spectacle as exciting as this, teachers and students collected densely about the door for a glimpse. Soon the news circulated through the campus that Ma Xiaolong dug through a wall to steal rice and the county police's German shepherd, following the scent, led the police straight to his bed.

After the discovery of the sack of rice and the three lunch boxes, the lean policeman led the dog, which had accomplished its mission in flying colors, back to the jeep. The fat policeman brought Ma Xiaolong to the principal's office. The lean policeman returned shortly, and the two policemen started to interrogate Ma Xiaolong, with Principal Pockmark listening in. The lean policeman readied pen and paper to record the interrogation.

The fat policeman asked, "What's your name?"

Ma Xiaolong said, trembling, "My name is Ma Xiaolong."

The fat policeman then asked, "How old are you?"

Ma Xiaolong said, "I am 15."

The fat policeman asked, "What's your father's name?"

Ma Xiaolong said, "My father's name is Ma Changsong."

The principal got up and went over to the fat policeman and whispered into his ear. Ma Xiaolong couldn't make out what was said, but he knew

Principal Pockmark was badmouthing his father. Maybe he mentioned his father's former service as army doctor in the Kuomintang troops and his alleged embezzlement of two thousand yuan.

The fat policeman kept nodding as the principal whispered; then he asked Ma Xiaolong, "Where did you go last night?"

Ma Xiaolong said, "I was sleeping in my room last night."

The fat policeman asked, "Didn't you go somewhere last night?"

Ma Xiaolong said, "I didn't go anywhere."

The fat policeman asked, "How did those items found under your bed get there then?"

Ma Xiaolong said, "I have no idea how they got there."

The fat policeman said, "Ma Xiaolong, I'm warning you. You must speak the truth to us. Your father is already in big trouble. You don't want to follow him there."

Now Ma Xiaolong knew what Principal Pockmark had whispered into the policeman's ear. He shot a glance at the principal and said, "I told you the truth."

The fat policeman said, "The truth my foot! If

you hadn't gone out last night, would the sack of rice have moved on its own power under your bed?"

Ma Xiaolong said, "I really didn't go out last night. I really was sleeping in my room."

The fat policeman said, "Who can confirm that you did not go out last night and was sleeping in your room?"

After considering a moment, Ma Xiaolong said, "Liu Tingsong sleeps across from me. He can corroborate that."

The fat policeman, the lean one and Principal Pockmark huddled together and consulted briefly in a subdued murmur. Then the lean policeman opened the door and left the room.

Principal Pockmark said with a sardonic laugh, "Three lunch boxes were found under your bed too. How do you explain that?"

Looking at the pimples on the principal's face, Ma Xiaolong stuttered, "I ....don't know ..."

Principal Pockmark said, "At the last morning assembly I already mentioned this matter without naming names, and I summoned you to my office for a talk. Do you remember? As a matter of fact I did not make an unsubstantiated accusation; I had received a letter denouncing you written by someone in your class some time back. I called you to my office in order to give you a chance to come clean, but you forfeited the chance. Today the county police have cracked the case. What do you have to say?"

Ma Xiaolong briefly moved his lips but did not know what to say. He lifted his head to look at the adults. He felt hemmed in like an insignificant insect. He wanted to cry but dared not do so, for fear of angering the principal. His aunt had warned him that Principal Pockmark hated crybabies.

The fat policeman, who had appeared indifferent so far, also lifted his head to give him a sharp look while muttering something. The lean policeman returned, pushing the door open and making a beeline for Ma Xiaolong. He fixed him with a fierce stare and blustered to the frail subject of interrogation, "You are a liar! Liu Tingsong said he saw you go out last night and was away for an hour!"

A cry of surprise escaped Ma Xiaolong's mouth and his face was distorted with fright. It never occurred to him that Liu Tingsong would frame him by lying. Blaming himself for this belated realization and desperate to protest his innocence, he cried, "He lied, he lied! I really didn't leave my room for one minute!"

The three adults exchanged looks. Then, Principal Pockmark shot a fierce glance at Ma Xiaolong, and a faint smile gathered on the faces of the two policemen.

An electric bell rang across the campus. Without needing to look at the clock, Ma Xiaolong knew, from a scattering of steps and voices and laughter, that it was time for the first class of the day. He said to Principal Pockmark, "I need to go to my class. There is a math quiz in the first class of the day."

Principal Pockmark said, "So you think you are going back to class, eh? With all that you have done, you think you'll be allowed to go back to your classes? I'll be frank with you: if it is proved that you stole rice from the storage room or that you stole the lunch boxes, if one of these proves to be true, I can expel you from the school."

The fat policeman held out a hand, palm down, and moved it downwards a few times, seemingly to cut the principal off, and said, "Yes, you want to go back to class. We want you to go back to class too. But if the matter is not cleared up, there's no way you'll be allowed to leave here. Let me tell you, kid. If you don't come clean about last night, then it's no longer a question of going back to class. It will be a question of handcuffing you and taking you to the county police headquarters."

The fat policeman accompanied the words with an emphatic bang of his hand on the table, startling Ma Xiaolong, who turned white as a sheet. He hadn't had any breakfast yet and was weak with hunger. His mouth felt dry and was giving off an unpleasant odor. He craved to gulp down that glass of cold water sitting on the principal's desk.

The sounds of teachers and students greeting each other in their classrooms came into earshot, through the hall, in waves of varying intensity. Soon the teachers began their lectures, in male or female voices spanning a range of registers. Chickens raised on nearby farms came onto the school grounds to grub for food under the window of the principal's office, making a rustling, scratching sound. The athletic field was now deserted, with only the late autumn sunlight playing on the grassy surface; a palpable quiet descended on the campus. Amid these sights and sounds, Ma Xiaolong was assailed by a sudden sense of emptiness, which was so overwhelming he felt like crying.

Principal Pockmark took a red pack of Peony cigarettes from a drawer, opened it and held out the pack to the policemen before lighting a cigarette for himself. The three adults were now having a convivial chat about the aromas of cigarettes, leaving Ma Xiaolong alone for the moment. There was an instant relaxation of the tension in the room. Ma Xiaolong had heard from his aunt that Principal Pockmark had a regular supply of fine cigarettes in red packs due to his official position. These Peony cigarettes in red packs must be what she was talking about, he thought. He sniffed a few times and found the smell of cigarette smoke quite pleasant; it was even unaccountably heart-warming and he wished they would go on smoking forever.

After a few drags on his cigarette, the fat policeman turned his gaze on Ma Xiaolong again and said, "Well? Still not ready to talk? What did you really do last night?"

Ma Xiaolong said, "I didn't do anything. I really was sleeping."

Principal Pockmark said, "Ma Xiaolong! It seems the only way to make you come clean is for me to explain in stark terms the dire situation you are in. Listen! Your father was arrested yesterday afternoon and remanded to the county prison. If you don't own up to your misdeeds, you are going to end up like your father. Is that what you want for yourself?"

Ma Xiaolong was dumbfounded and had a sense of having fallen from a precipice. His head started throbbing. He couldn't believe his father had really been thrown in prison! His face first turned red, then pale again, even paler than before. His lips gradually turned black, in sharp contrast to the pallor of his face, a paleness that was bluish gray, a paleness seen only on a death mask.

All three adults fixed their eyes on Ma Xiaolong. There was an icy hardness in their stare, hardly the kind normally adopted with an adolescent. Ma Xiaolong felt his heart being stabbed to pieces by their stares. He said, "I was really sleeping in my room last night. I really didn't do anything ..."

As he said this, Ma Xiaolong thought of his father, his back curled like a shrimp under a dim light. He was heartbroken and began weeping noisily in front of the three grown men.

4

That same day Ma Xiaolong fell ill.

When Principal Pockmark learned of his illness, he summoned Teacher Jin, the class teacher of Class

6 of Ninth Grade, and asked without preliminaries, "Are you aware that your student Ma Xiaolong has fallen ill?"

Teacher Jin said, "Yes, I know."

Principal Pockmark said, "Is the illness genuine or faked?"

Teacher Jin said, "The illness can hardly be faked. He has sunk into a deep sleep and is running a high temperature. He had spasms and was talking nonsense."

Principal Pockmark said, "Talking nonsense? What did he say?"

Teacher Jin said, "I didn't pay attention. I guess it was some childish nonsense." Principal Pockmark said, as his face acquired a stern expression, "You're so naïve! You are not vigilant enough. This serious incident on our campus has sent a seismic wave through the county education system. The police are keeping a close watch on this. I don't think Ma Xiaolong can come out of this unscathed."

Teacher Jin said, "Ma Xiaolong has a timid temperament. It's unlike him to have such temerity."

Principal Pockmark said, "Again this shows your bookish naiveté. What do you mean he doesn't seem the type to have such temerity? It's more complicated than you think. It's not easy for us adults to know what kids are up to. Can you really vouch for Ma Xiaolong's innocence?"

Teacher Jin said, "I made a discreet inquiry and found Ma Xiaolong would not have had the time to perpetrate the alleged acts."

Principal Pockmark said, "He had the time to do it. Didn't Liu Tingsong say Ma Xiaolong was more than an hour absent from the dorm room last night?"

Teacher Jin said, "Liu Tingsong's statement cannot be trusted. He has always nursed a grudge against Ma Xiaolong. I talked to Liu Tingsong. I asked him when Ma Xiaolong's one-hour absence commenced and when it ended. He was evasive in his answer and finally gave the times as from 11 p.m. to midnight. I immediately knew he was fabricating. I was on night duty last night and in the period he said Ma Xiaolong was absent, I was making the rounds to check on the students to see if they were in bed. I saw with my own eyes that Ma Xiaolong was fast asleep in his bed at that time; there's no way he could have been the one who stole rice from the storage room."

Principal Pockmark said, "Whose bed did you find to be unoccupied then?"

Teacher Jin said, "All students were accounted for."

Principal Pockmark said, "How do you explain the fact that the police dog sent from the county sniffed out Ma Xiaolong and not someone else? And the dog ferreted out both the sack of rice and the three lunch boxes. How do you explain that?"

Teacher Jin said, "I can't explain it. I merely want to say that Liu Tingsong's statement about Ma Xiaolong's one-hour absence from his room last night was simply not true."

Principal Pockmark said, waving his hand, "All right, all right! Let's not dwell on this. Tell me, do you know about the case involving Ma Xiaolong's father, Ma Changsong?"

Teacher Jin said, "Yes, I do."

Principal Pockmark said, "So you know. That's why we attach such importance to parental influence. You are a class teacher, so you need to sharpen your eyes and look at things from the perspective of class struggle. The father Ma Changsong embezzled public funds and the son committed thefts. Like father like son. It shouldn't surprise you."

Teacher Jin looked across at Principal Pockmark in astonishment, he moved his lips but didn't say anything, thinking to himself: According to your logic, there's not a good person in the Ma household.

If that is so, why have you been so intimate with his sister-in-law? Do you really think people are unaware of your hanky-panky with Ms. Zheng the school doctor?

Principal Pockmark brought out a pack of cigarettes and offered one to Teacher Jin, who declined. He lit one for himself and began smoking; he said, "What I mean is we must consider the far-reaching implications of this incident involving Ma Xiaolong. We mustn't be blinded by pity for this little boy. We need to assign a student to stay with him and hear what nonsense he spouts. This may help detect inconsistencies and uncover clues that will help solve the case. What do you say, Teacher Jin?"

Teacher Jin said, "It's your decision."

Principal Pockmark said, "Good! Liu Tingsong in your class will be a good choice for the task. Since he sleeps across from Ma Xiaolong in the dorm, no suspicion is likely to be aroused if we say he is there to take care of a patient. What do you say?"

Teacher Jin had no alternative but to go back to his class and assign the task to Liu Tingsong. He explained to Liu Tingsong that his task consisted mainly of attending to the daily needs of Ma Xiaolong, such as bringing him meals and drinking water from the school refectory and opening the window to air the room. The gathering of information was secondary and done only as the opportunity presented itself. Liu Tingsong was overjoyed because he always hated attending classes and now he had received an unexpected errand from the principal and the class teacher. With a shrill whistle he disappeared like a whiff of smoke in the direction of the dorm.

As he ran toward the dorm, he was considering various ways of making an intimidating first impression on Ma Xiaolong. Just before he reached the dorm, a smirk appeared on his face. He turned his body sideways, set his jaw and kicked at the door with full force. The sudden thunderous noise so startled and frightened Ma Xiaolong that he flipped like a fish and sat up with a jolt on his bed. He turned his eyes toward the door in great consternation, his face suddenly blanched, looking as if driven witless. Seeing the effect his appearance produced, Liu Tingsong, suppressing his mirth, sashayed facetiously to the bed and deliberately brought his face close to Ma Xiaolong, as if to look at a painting, before throwing back his head and breaking into a fit of cackling laughter.

Ma Xiaolong, weakened by illness, had a blank

look in his eyes. He got down from his bed to fetch a cup, but when he picked up the thermos to pour himself some water; he found it empty. Liu Tingsong snatched the bottle from him and made for the door, saying in a raised voice over his shoulder, "I have been sent here to serve you water and tea!"

Liu Tingsong filled half of the bottle with boiling water at the water station behind the refectory and headed back, but took a detour to the latrine first. He checked every stall to make sure there was nobody in it before pulling down his pants, uncorking the thermos and aiming a stream of urine at its mouth. Thanks to his accurate calculation, when he was done, the foam of his urine just came to the mouth of the bottle. Another smirk crossed his face as he replaced the cork on the thermos.

The water was poured into Ma Xiaolong's cup. Liu Tingsong fetched an enamel bowl and started pouring the water back and forth between the cup and the bowl. He observed that this would cool down the water much faster. Ma Xiaolong looked gratefully at Liu Tingsong. Following the cooling maneuver, Liu Tingsong handed the water to Ma Xiaolong. After taking two mouthfuls of the water, Ma Xiaolong suddenly furrowed his brow and said, smacking his lips, "This water tastes funny."

Liu Tingsong said, "Funny how?"

Ma Xiaolong said, "It tastes a little salty. The color is off too."

Liu Tingsong said, "It's so like you to be paranoid. Do you really think I'd poison your drink? The most likely explanation is that the refectory mixed the hot drinking water with the water left over from steaming rice."

Ma Xiaolong was reduced to silence and with a sheepish smile picked up the cup of water and, tilting back his head, gulped it down.

After learning of Ma Xiaolong's falling ill, Zheng Xiuli the school doctor hurried to the dorm during lunch break. She found a disheveled, haggard Ma Xiaolong, markedly wizened by the illness and her eyes began to moisten. She sat down at the head of Ma Xiaolong's bed and felt his forehead with her hand to check his temperature. The soft, light touch of her hand was warm and smooth like a hot air mass blowing across a river. With that touch, all the ill feeling toward his aunt evaporated in an instant and tears of misery started streaming down his face to fall onto the pillow.

Ma Xiaolong said, "Auntie ... I did not steal

anything, honest ..."

Zheng Xiuli said, "I know. Our Xiaolong does not steal."

Ma Xiaolong continued, "Auntie, father was put in prison ... did you know?"

Zheng Xiuli said, "Yes, I knew."

Ma Xiaolong said, "Father was wrongly accused."

Zheng Xiuli said, "I know ..."

The school doctor teared up as she said this. She quickly turned aside and got out a handkerchief to dry her eyes. Before leaving, she left a small bag of biscuits, saying, "Auntie bought these for you. They are saltines. Enjoy!"

But the moment she stepped out of the room Liu Tingsong grabbed the biscuits. Munching on the biscuits with obvious enjoyment, he said to Ma Xiaolong, "The illness must have killed your appetite. Cramming them down is bad for your health. I'll eat them for you."

Ma Xiaolong closed his eyes but the sound of Liu Tingsong crunching on the biscuits flooded his ears like an incoming tide and his saliva spewed like a geyser. Ma Xiaolong felt his viscera suddenly awakened. He started to perspire profusely and hunger went, like a wolf, on a rampage in his empty stomach and intestines.

After finishing off the biscuits, Liu Tingsong stripped himself naked and burrowed into his quilt. Then he beckoned Ma Xiaolong with a hooked index finger sticking out of the quilt, "Come sleep with me."

Ma Xiaolong looked with revulsion at the index finger and said, "I am going to study for a bit more."

Liu Tingsong's eyebrows shot up, his eyes glaring as he said with venom, "I dare you to do it!"

There was a sudden hush following these words. Ma Xiaolong dreaded any further eye contact with Liu Tingsong, as if Liu Tingsong were looking daggers at him. He timidly got up from his bed and crossed to Liu Tingsong's bedside.

Liu Tingsong lifted a corner of his quilt and gestured with his eyes for Ma Xiaolong to lie down next to him.

With all the fat on his plump body, Liu Tingsong had warmed his quilt nicely, but the moment Ma Xiaolong got into the quilt, he began shaking uncontrollably. He didn't want to have any physical contact with Liu Tingsong, considering it as dirty and slimy as a dead snake. But just as he edged away, Liu Tingsong shot out an arm and put it around him.

Liu Tingsong said, "Come! Let me feel you."

Ma Xiaolong said, "No!"

Liu Tingsong said, "I'll let you feel me too, all right?"

With that, Liu Tingsong got hold of Ma Xiaolong's hand and pulled it toward his private parts. Ma Xiaolong resisted and freed his hand from Liu Tingsong's grip and kept it doggedly close to his chest. He did not turn to face Liu Tingsong, but the latter put a strong hand on his shoulder and forcibly thrust the other toward his groin, allowing for no refusal.

Ma Xiaolong let out a cry and curled up like a shrimp.

A note or two of birdsong sounded outside the window. The bellows in the refectory kitchen started its rumble. From the public address system of West Town Elementary School blared forth the refrains of *Let's Pull the Oars*, broadcast like a cloud of colored confetti, swirling and dancing through the air.

Ma Xiaolong's cheeks twitched unstoppably; Liu Tingsong hurt him badly. Liu Tingsong's groping hand felt like the jaws of a ferocious dog; once they closed on the prey, there was no shaking them off. Just when he was plunged into suffocating despair, he felt Liu Tingsong's chest pressed into his back and something hard as a wooden stick was thrust between his thighs ...

Ma Xiaolong wept, but soundlessly, as teardrops fell freely from his closed eyes.

After his gymnastics in the bed for the best part of an afternoon, Liu Tingsong finally got exhausted and fell off, like a dead pig, into a deep sleep accompanied by noisy snoring. Ma Xiaolong on the other hand was wracked by fits of cold sweat, and sleep eluded him. He was hurting from Liu Tingsong's mauling and the bed sheet was grossly soiled. He couldn't stand it any longer and got up out of the bed in which Liu Tingsong slept like a top. As he put on his clothes, he looked with disgust at the obscene prone figure in the bed. A gleam of venom shot out from his eyes.

In the three days of Ma Xiaolong's house arrest in the dorm, Liu Tingsong kept up the same routine.

When he was not busy with this routine, Liu Tingsong did not forget to go to the principal's office to give periodic reports to Principal Pockmark about people who came to visit Ma Xiaolong and what they said. After listening attentively to his accounts, Principal Pockmark was full of praise for him, "You are truly a good student. Vigilance is crucial at a time like this. Without vigilance, you are as good as blind.

Do you understand?"

Liu Tingsong said, "I understand, Principal."

Principal Pockmark said, "You play an important role. Play it well! Keep Ma Xiaolong isolated. Deny him access to outside contacts. Things could get thorny if the bad eggs were allowed a chance to communicate and coordinate among themselves."

Liu Tingsong said, "Got it, Principal."

Principal Pockmark continued, "Is Ma Xiaolong still talking nonsense these days?"

Liu Tingsong said, "He's come down to earth. He no longer talks nonsense."

After a brief pause for reflection, Principal Pockmark asked Liu Tingsong, "Have you been recruited into the Communist Youth League?"

Liu Tingsong said, "Not yet. I don't get any recognition in Teacher Jin's class."

Principal Pockmark said, "What's the matter with Teacher Jin? I'll talk to him. The Youth League needs students like you."

Liu Tingsong nodded vigorously, his eyebrows arched in excitement.

Principal Pockmark said, "You must strive hard to qualify for the League, understand? In these crucial days especially, you'd do well to cultivate greater vigilance and maintain surveillance of the actions and words of Ma Xiaolong. If with your help the county police solve the case, it would count as a great merit in your favor. I, as principal, will then naturally recommend you for the League, agreed?"

Liu Tingsong was elated. The moment the principal turned to leave, he turned a few cartwheels in the corridor.

The food offered in the refectory was getting worse. When the students complained, Fatso Xu and his co-workers in the kitchen blamed it on thieves. Fatso Xu said, "The theft of rice from our storage room has added to our difficulty. The rice inventory is already closely monitored to the smallest unit of weight. With the theft, we now have a gaping hole." The students said, "Didn't the county police dog ferret out the stolen rice from under Ma Xiaolong's bed? What other holes are you talking about?" Fatso Xu said, "Who knows how much rice was stolen? The dog only brought out one bag of rice; who knows how many more bags were taken?" The students said, "Doesn't the refectory management keep a record of the inventory?" Fatso Xu offered a faltering, unconvincing reply. The students were led to suspect that there had always been irregularities on the books of the refectory management; the theft could presumably have given the management an opportunity to cover up and rationalize the previous gaps and shortfalls.

On the pretext of bringing meals to Ma Xiaolong, Liu Tingsong always took two portions from Luo Zhaoying. He would finish eating his own portion in the refectory before ensconcing himself in a quiet spot away from prying eyes and eating the greater part of Ma Xiaolong's portion. He gave the little that was left over to Ma Xiaolong, without forgetting to pause in a shadowy part of the corridor and spit into the food. Ma Xiaolong, who was dizzy from hunger, never suspected any mischief and would scarf down the food in no time, thanking Liu Tingsong profusely afterwards.

But no secret is safe forever. Sure he'd impeccably hidden the tracks of his predations of Ma Xiaolong's meals, Liu Tingsong was surprised in the act one day by Luo Zhaoying, who was turning a corner in the dorm building.

Luo Zhaoying gave a startled look while Liu Tingsong froze momentarily, his mouth full of food. Neither spoke, but smart girl that she was,

Luo Zhaoying instantly understood the unspeakable enormity perpetrated by the other. The portion allotted to each student was already piteously paltry, she thought, how was Ma Xiaolong supposed to survive on the much reduced ration left over after Liu Tingsong took a big bite out of it?

Luo Zhaoying finished her meal distractedly. She kept imagining Ma Xiaolong's eyes—slightly protruding, big and bright, shrewd yet timid, their clarity suffused with sadness, not the eyes of the average teenage boy, but rather of a ravaged woman.

Luo Zhaoying sighed; she truly felt sorry for Ma Xiaolong. That morning word spread on campus that the county police dog headed straight to the boys' dormitory and zeroed in on Ma Xiaolong of Class 6 of Ninth Grade. She could imagine how terrified he must have been. People were saying that Ma Xiaolong was the thief, the burglar, who stole the day students' lunch boxes as well as rice from the storage room … When she heard it, Luo Zhaoying felt and heard blood rush into her head with a roar. She would never believe Ma Xiaolong could be a thief. Ma Xiaolong was known for his timidity and brains. He enjoyed studying, eating and playing and got along well with his school fellows. He got visibly nervous whenever the teacher's voice was even slightly raised. He was more the type that worried about a falling leaf for fear that it would injure his skull. Besides, in all these years of studying together and living in close proximity, she had never heard of any instance of stealing involving Ma Xiaolong. How could a student like him have stooped so low as to steal lunch boxes from day students or break into the rice store at such risk to himself?

Then word spread that Ma Xiaolong adamantly denied the thefts. Luo Zhaoying greeted the news with private support for Ma Xiaolong, directed at Ma Xiaolong's empty chair in the classroom: Well done, Ma Xiaolong! Never back down!

At the morning assembly the following day, Principal Pockmark referred to the matter in front of the staff and students of the entire school. Luo Zhaoying sensed that the case had not yet been nailed shut! Principal Pockmark, significantly, did not say the county police had solved the case, nor did he name Ma Xiaolong. He called the meeting for the express purpose of encouraging the faculty and student body, particularly Class 6 of Ninth Grade and the boarding students, to step up with information and clues that might help expose the perpetrator and crack this case. It was obvious that the perpetrator he alluded to could only be Ma Xiaolong. He demanded that the perpetrator be watched strictly and held incommunicado to prevent unauthorized contacts; that staff and students heighten their vigilance and sever any association with the perpetrator. He went on to warn that the school administration would deal harsh punishment to anyone found to have any dealings with or pass information to the perpetrator.

Luo Zhaoying only learned after the fact that Liu Tingsong had been exempted from attending classes and assigned to keep watch on Ma Xiaolong in his dorm room. Liu Tingsong's surveillance over Ma Xiaolong reminded her of the proverbial weasel guarding a hen house. After surprising Liu Tingsong in the act of furtively taking a big bite out of Ma Xiaolong's meal, she had an even lower opinion of Liu Tingsong and greater concerns about Ma Xiaolong's plight. She was determined to check in on Ma Xiaolong as soon as there was a chance to do so.

One day at noontime Liu Tingsong went to the refectory for lunch, leaving Ma Xiaolong alone in his dorm room. Lying on his bed, he suddenly heard a hissing sound and saw a small white ball fly in through the window. Startled, Ma Xiaolong looked out the window but saw no one. He bent down to pick up the projectile and found it to be a piece of paper crumpled into a ball. He opened it to read:

"Ma Xiaolong,

"Don't give in to pressure! You did not commit any theft; don't allow anybody to pressure you into backing down!

"A girl who has abiding faith in you"

Ma Xiaolong went back to the window to look out. It was a cloudless day; the early winter sun shone softly; the willow twigs with a few lonely yellowed leaves that had not separated and fallen swayed gently in the breeze. A convoy of boats sailed past on the Town River, their diesel engines rumbling and their steam whistles mooing like cows.

He had fleeting glimpses of the face of a student in the sunlit bushes. Ma Xiaolong tried attentively to capture that face, his body becoming hot and dry as if it were on fire. He stuffed the note under his pillow but couldn't help taking it out time and again to read it over. His heart, like a bird flapping its wings, flew out the window, soared into the sky and he imagined himself surrounded by the cheerful laughter he had longed for ...

5

That note Luo Zhaoying lobbed into his room was like a shining star streaking across the night sky. Ma Xiaolong's body miraculously recovered its strength overnight and the tension in his head lessened. With the regaining of his strength, however, he began to feel hungrier and the pangs of hunger became more intense.

As hunger gnawed at his entrails, Ma Xiaolong pined for the tidbits he used to savor, particularly that bag of peanuts he had flung onto the floor that night to spite his aunt. He imagined the exquisite pleasure he would have had when he dropped the peanuts into his mouth one at a time, chewing and savoring them at leisure; if only he still had that bag of peanuts!

After much consideration, while lying in his bed, he finally made up his mind to put it to Liu Tingsong: he wanted to take his meals in the refectory instead of being served in his dorm room. He had a creeping suspicion that his meal portions were shrinking and Liu Tingsong might have something to do with it. Besides, he wanted to see Luo Zhaoying. He had never yearned as much as now to be with her.

One day at noontime, after returning to his

room from washing his and Liu Tingsong's bowls, he said, with his back to Liu Tingsong, "I'm going to the refectory to have my meal this evening."

Liu Tingsong lifted his head and stared at his back in astonishment, as if he were someone he was meeting for the first time.

Ma Xiaolong kept his back turned to Liu Tingsong as he said, "I've recovered my strength now. I can't continue to bother you with the chores of bringing my food and drink."

Liu Tingsong rested his eyes on Ma Xiaolong's back for a few seconds before he gave a laugh and said, "Very well, suits me perfectly if you want to take your meals at the refectory. I'm fed up with bringing your meals every day."

Ma Xiaolong breathed a long sigh of relief and turned around to smile timidly at Liu Tingsong.

Liu Tingsong said, "But on one condition."

Ma Xiaolong said, "What's the condition?"

Liu Tingsong said with a mysterious smile, "Not now. I'll tell you later."

Liu Tingsong stripped himself naked and got under his quilt. He motioned Ma Xiaolong to his bedside and told him to kneel down; then he forcefully bent Ma Xiaolong's head down toward his groin.

...

The bell for the evening meal finally sounded, and Ma Xiaolong picked up his bowl and chopsticks, all set to leave. His eyes brightened at the thought of being able to see Luo Zhaoying soon. He left all the humiliation he had been subjected to and all the unpleasant memories behind him.

It was at this moment that Liu Tingsong got back from the latrine. Once in the room, he directed a derisive laugh at Ma Xiaolong and, with a flick of his sordid index finger across Ma Xiaolong's chin, said, "So you want to take your meals in the refectory! Don't even think about it! Before the rice storage theft is solved, you'll not leave this room by orders of the principal himself!"

Ma Xiaolong was dumbfounded. Watching Liu Tingsong swagger out of the room and hearing a clanking noise as he locked the door, Ma Xiaolong flopped onto his bed.

Sometime after that he heard an unusual noise coming from outside the door. Ma Xiaolong asked warily, "Who is it?"

There was no answer. Then he suddenly saw a form jump in through the window. Ma Xiaolong cried in astonishment, "Luo Zhaoying!"

Luo Zhaoying put a finger to her lips, signaling him to be quiet.

Ma Xiaolong asked, "Why are you here?"

Luo Zhaoying answered, "I'm here to see you."

Ma Xiaolong said, "That's not a good idea! Go now! If Liu Tingsong comes back this minute and sees you here, there will be big trouble!"

Luo Zhaoying said, "If I am not afraid of that, why should you be?"

Ma Xiaolong said, "The county police suspect me of having broken into the rice storage and you'll implicate yourself if you are found here."

Luo Zhaoying said, "Implicate myself? If I were afraid of getting implicated, I wouldn't have written you that note. Did you read that note?"

Ma Xiaolong said, "I read it."

Luo Zhaoying said, "That's good. Others may believe you are the rice thief, but I don't! Promise me that you did not do it!"

Ma Xiaolong looked the girl in the eye and said clearly and earnestly, "I did not do it!"

Luo Zhaoying said, "Good! I believe you."

Ma Xiaolong nodded, a big teardrop quietly rolling down his cheek.

Luo Zhaoying said, "Has Liu Tingsong been

abusing you these days?"

Ma Xiaolong gave a startled look, then shook his head.

Luo Zhaoying said, "He did abuse you, didn't he?"

Ma Xiaolong shook his head vigorously and answered with a string of "no's," thinking at the same time: Liu Tingsong is an evil spirit taking possession of me. But that kind of thing is unmentionable.

Luo Zhaoying said, "There's no need to keep it a secret. Even I know that Liu Tingsong is the type to stab you in the back."

She was on the point of telling him about Liu Tingsong's stealing part of his meals but checked herself. She said, "You must have starved these past days."

Ma Xiaolong said, "I didn't have a great appetite anyway because of my illness. But starting yesterday my appetite has come back ..."

Luo Zhaoying placed a cloth sack on Ma Xiaolong's bed and said, "This is a bag of yams from home. They are cooked. You can have some when you feel hungry."

Ma Xiaolong said, "But your family does not have enough food either ..."

Luo Zhaoying said, her tone heightened with impatience, "Under the circumstance, do I look like I'm doing this only out of civility?"

At this, Ma Xiaolong lowered his head. He could smell a sweet, rich aroma of yams oozing out of the bag and washing over his heart like sunshine on green grass on an autumn day. He took a deep sniffle and a funny rumble rose from some part in his intestines, as if in dialogue with him. A sudden sadness came over him and tears welled up in his eyes. To hide them from Luo Zhaoying, he averted his face and let the tears roll down his cheeks unobserved. The tears bounced off his chest to land on his pillow.

None of this escaped Luo Zhaoying's notice. There was a quiver in her heart and a warm wave rose in her chest; she reached out and gently took Ma Xiaolong's hands into her own.

Surrounding sounds in the dorm building seemed all of a sudden to recede and a fraught silence descended around them. As the two adolescents held each other's eyes everything appeared to coalesce. Their cheeks were in flame and their breath quickened and became heavy as if they were on a brisk run. The air in the room felt burning on their skin because of their heavy breathing.

Ma Xiaolong looked down at Luo Zhaoying's hands. Those were familiar hands, hands that exhibited such grace and delicacy as they held the rice bowl in the refectory. The almost translucent texture of those hands against the sunlight had left an indelible impression on him. In retrospect, the fantasy of touching these hands probably dated back a long time. Now those hands were joined with his in real life! What's more, her fingers were gently stroking his palms, as if communicating something to him, telling him something ...

Ma Xiaolong's heart was brimming with warm blood, rushing, as it were, up to his throat. This was the first time he ever held a girl's hand for such a long spell. Other than his mother, no member of the opposite sex had ever held his hand so lovingly. He felt his hand grow instantly bigger in her grip, and somewhat numb. He shuddered as if he'd had an electric shock. He felt the warm, smooth softness of Luo Zhaoying's hands and was acutely aware of the profuse sweating of his own hands ...

Ma Xiaolong's blood raced and his heart beat like an arrhythmic roll of a drum. He looked away to avoid Luo Zhaoying's eyes, but he couldn't avoid the overpowering sensation in his hands. He felt a thinning and lightening of his heart and his body was on the point of soaring into the air. There was a sudden awakening in the depth of his lower abdomen: Something was heating up, swelling and soon developing into a boiling molten liquid that sloshed around inside a tin can. Then, in only seconds, the tin can exploded with a boom, and the burning liquid spewed forth in rhythmic spurts ...

Luo Zhaoying stared at Ma Xiaolong in astonishment and asked, shaking his hands, "What happened to you?"

Ma Xiaolong had turned white as a sheet and sweat poured down his back. He looked away in a fluster and murmured, "It's nothing, nothing ..."

Suddenly they became aware of the sound of someone opening the door lock. Ma Xiaolong's face blanched; shaking off Luo Zhaoying's hands, he exclaimed in a low voice, "He's here!"

Luo Zhaoying did not lose her composure, but picked up Ma Xiaolong's hand and gave it a few light shakes before pushing open the window and agilely jumping out. As Ma Xiaolong got up to close the window, Luo Zhaoying waved her hand outside the window and quietly closed it for him.

Liu Tingsong came into the room and crossed to

Ma Xiaolong's bed. Sniffing the air, he asked, "What happened? I seem to smell the odor of a third person."

Ma Xiaolong said, "What third person?"

Liu Tingsong said, "Was someone here?"

Ma Xiaolong said, "How could that be? Didn't you lock the door?" Liu Tingsong, unconvinced, cast a glance at Ma Xiaolong before crossing to the window to scan the surroundings.

A wind rose and the leafless tree branches swayed in the frigid air. An occasional yellowed leaf, borne on the wind, was slapped against the window pane, where it stayed momentarily before being blown away by another gust of wind.

Ma Xiaolong had thought he had recovered his strength. But the following day he caught a cold again and the fever came back.

It happened all because of an accident at the latrine: when he got up to buckle up his pants, his wallet fell with a splash into the hole in the floor.

He let out a cry of alarm. Liu Tingsong, who was standing guard outside the latrine, said, "What are you hollering for? What's the fuss about?"

Ma Xiaolong said, "My wallet fell into the hole!"

Liu Tingsong said, "So what? How much money

could you have in it?"

Ma Xiaolong fell silent. A clammy, cold sweat broke out on his back. He forgot if he had two or three dimes in it, but he did clearly remember he had a total of three *jin*'s worth (one *jin* is about half a kilogram) of staple food ration coupons: two *jin* of province-issued coupons and one-*jin* national coupon.

Luo Zhaoying, had discreetly given him the one-*jin* national staple food coupon a few months ago, telling him, "This is a national food coupon. You must use it sparingly. It is much more valuable than a province-issue coupon because you can use it in any part of the country. With it, you won't go hungry even if you are in Beijing. A one-*jin* national food coupon is worth five *jin* of province-issue coupons." Luo Zhaoying reminded Ma Xiaolong that the national coupon could also be redeemed for cooking oil in the staple food stores. Armed with the one-*jin* national food coupon, Ma Xiaolong felt instantly enabled. In the days that followed, he would take out that coupon and study it closely every night before bed. The more he studied it the more impressed he was by its rare value. Look at it! It's not tiny like the provincial coupons—those were the size of the pad of a finger, in flimsy paper too, and the stamp marks on them were anemic. This national food coupon, true to its name, was classy, the size of a one-fen note (one fen is about 0.16 cent), and crisp like a freshly minted bill. It had heft in one's hand; it was fancily printed and when he glided a finger across it, he could feel the fine embossing on its surface; on the back were printed a list of instructions, among which figured all the benefits explained to him by Luo Zhaoying ... Ah! I, Ma Xiaolong, am finally in possession of a national staple food coupon!

But now this one-*jin* national coupon and the two-*jin* provincial coupon, as well as the few dimes in his wallet had all gone down the hole! Ma Xiaolong was panic-stricken. He felt a sudden sinking of his heart followed by a tightening of his throat. He was drained empty in an instant. He felt as if in a dream. Staring at the wallet afloat in the fecal waste, he had a strong urge to dive in for it.

The wallet was not what you'd imagine a wallet to be, but one made by folding thick sketch paper. Quite a few students in his class had wallets made of paper; only those whose families were well off could afford to buy leather wallets in department stores. Luo Zhaoying was considered the best crafter of paper wallets in her class. With her lovely hands deftly folding two pieces of sketch paper this way and that way, a smart-looking wallet was born. To Ma Xiaolong's mind, those two hands working with the sketch paper were like a pair of butterflies flitting among flowers. It was Luo Zhaoying who taught him to make his own wallet.

Ma Xiaolong made up his mind to fish out the wallet from the latrine as soon as possible, knowing that any delay would mean the sketch paper would be saturated with the fecal waste water and sink to the bottom. It would be very difficult then to try and salvage it.

He ran out of the outhouse like a whirlwind, startling Liu Tingsong, who was guarding the door. Liu Tingsong waved his hands in the air, yelling after him, but Ma Xiaolong seemed not to have heard him. He broke into a sprint; anyone spotting this running figure would not have believed he was ill. The school cesspit was very large and held a huge amount of fecal waste; it was an important source of fertilizer for the production brigades nearby. It was mostly open to the sky, with only a tiny part enclosed in an outhouse. When Ma Xiaolong reached the open pit, he immediately spotted his wallet, a white object still afloat on the surface of the fecal waste.

Because of the food shortage, the human excrement ending up in the pit was as thin and insubstantial as the food on the table. Ma Xiaolong could see that the pool was greenish with undigested vegetable fiber that bore little resemblance to feces. He extended a hand toward the wallet but it was beyond his reach. He cast about, desperately searching for a solution. He found a dead branch and stretched it out as far as he could to nudge the wallet toward dry land. He was extremely nervous, fearing that too much force might cause the wallet to sink. He gingerly and slowly coaxed the thing toward him until finally the paper wallet was once again safely in his hand. In a moment of elation, his feet slipped and he fell into the cesspit with a splash and found himself submerged up to his waist.

Ma Xiaolong clambered as best he could out of the pit. He felt neither regret nor vexation. When he opened the sodden wallet saturated with fecal waste and took out the paper bills and food ration coupons, he found both the provincial food ration coupons and the one-dime bills soggy and limp, while the one-*jin* national food ration coupon alone was still crisp and smart, and its colors were even brighter than before its baptism in human waste. He couldn't help muttering in admiration: it's a national ration coupon after all!

Liu Tingsong lost no time in spreading among his classmates the news of Ma Xiaolong's fall into the cesspit, which he considered very amusing. Only Luo Zhaoying knew the reason behind Ma Xiaolong's desperate effort to retrieve the wallet.

Ma Xiaolong was oblivious of all that was going on. He was busy changing and washing his soiled clothes in the icy bathroom, and cleaning himself up. He rinsed off the paper bills and the food ration coupons, patted off the excess moisture with a towel and stuck them on the window pane to dry. Gusts of cold wind blew into the room and the icy water reddened his hands. But in the excitement of a treasure lost and found again, the cold was the last thing on his mind.

That day Ma Xiaolong ran a fever again.

But Liu Tingsong was not letting Ma Xiaolong off the hook. In the afternoon, after the other boarders left the dorm for their classes, he extended a hand from under his quilt and beckoned, with his index finger, at the feverish Ma Xiaolong.

This time Ma Xiaolong ignored him.

Liu Tingsong said with a laugh, "Since you don't

want to come to my bed, I'll come to yours."

And he threw off his quilt and jumped, naked, into Ma Xiaolong's bed.

6

That very afternoon Huanglou Township Secondary School was rocked by the shocking news that Ma Xiaolong, of Class 6 of Ninth Grade, armed with a fruit knife, stabbed a much taller classmate to death in his bed!

The county police came back in force, but this time without the big dog. Clearly the dog was not needed because it was an open-and-shut case; the killer was Ma Xiaolong.

Moments before he was put into the police car, Ma Xiaolong spotted Luo Zhaoying among the onlookers. Luo Zhaoying saw a momentary pause in Ma Xiaolong's walk to the car, his lips twitching as if he had something to say to her. His face was ashen and he had acquired black circles around his eyes, which made his eyes appear doubly big and doubly deep-set.

Luo Zhaoying covered her face and started to cry.

To everyone's surprise, Teacher Jin, the class teacher of Class 6 of Ninth Grade, soon went to the county government and volunteered to be Ma Xiaolong's defender in court. He told the authorities with jurisdiction over the case that after the incident he had a conversation with Ma Xiaolong. He had solid evidence that the deceased Liu Tingsong was a juvenile delinquent who had sexually abused Ma Xiaolong. He pointed out that the stabbing of Liu Tingsong was in fact an act of self-defense on the part of Ma Xiaolong, who could no longer bear the sexual predations. Of course the question of whether the self-defense was excessive would be argued in court.

The case dragged on without a date set for trial. It was said that in all the years since Liberation this kind of crime involving juveniles had been unheard-of, not only in the county, but also in the province, and even in the whole country.

One day, half a year later, a policeman in the juvenile correction facility told Ma Xiaolong that his sister was there to see him.

It was a total surprise to Ma Xiaolong, who came out of his cell with doubt in his mind. In the visitors' room, he saw a woman with a pleasant figure standing with her back to him, her face lifted, reading a poster entitled "Instructions for Family Visitors," hung high on a wall. At the sound of Ma Xiaolong's approaching footsteps, the woman turned her head around.

Ma Xiaolong moved his lips and blurted out the three syllables "Luo—Zhao—Ying."

Luo Zhaoying was now a freshman in a magnet provincial high school. Despite the metal grille separating the visitor from the inmate, she took Ma Xiaolong's hand into her own, as she had done before. She held Ma Xiaolong's eyes as tears welled up in her eyes.

She brought Ma Xiaolong a few pieces of news.

The first was that Ma Xiaolong's father had died in prison a few days before; the rumor circulating in the school was that he was driven to suicide by guilt.

The second was, Zheng Xiuli, Ma Xiaolong's aunt, had filed for divorce and was soon to marry Principal Pockmark.

The third was, the case of the robbery of the school's rice store had been cracked. The case was not solved as a result of any investigation by the county police, but as a byproduct of a separate case being solved. When the offender of that case made a full confession. The criminal, a classmate of Liu

Tingsong's in elementary school, admitted to the
county police that it was he and Liu Tingsong who
broke into the rice store; he loaded the stolen rice
on a boat and sold it in a neighboring county, with
half of the proceeds going to Liu Tingsong. It was
also Liu Tingsong's idea to plant the bag of rice and
the aluminum lunch boxes under Ma Xiaolong's bed.
When he did it, Liu Tingsong had on Ma Xiaolong's
shoes and kept repeating, "I'm going to make Ma
Xiaolong pay with his life."

Ma Xiaolong stared at Luo Zhaoying, his Adam's
apple rising and falling a few times as he emitted a
strange sound. After a long silence, a sudden shiver
ran through his body and he tried to draw his hands
back through the grille, but Luo Zhaoying held them
in a tight grip, refusing to let go.

Luo Zhaoying also told Ma Xiaolong that in
order to help with his defense, Teacher Jin had taken
the train to the provincial capital, where he was going
to consult a relative who taught at the Institute of
Political Science and Law. Before setting off, Teacher
Jin vowed that he would defend this student of his
to the end, even if he risked being fired by Principal
Pockmark.

A big round teardrop appeared first in one then

in another of his deep-set eyes. Luo Zhaoying could see clearly that the two teardrops were black! She could feel that Ma Xiaolong's hands were shaking all this time. She was certain that in these months Ma Xiaolong's hands had not grown but rather had shrunk. His palms felt ice-cold and she had not succeeded in warming them up by holding them in her hands for over half an hour!

Ma Xiaolong did not say a word throughout the visit. Only when, at the end of the visit, Luo Zhaoying watched him disappear into the maws of the prison did she hear a blood-curdling howl from behind the ice-cold wrought iron bars.

Stories by Contemporary Writers from Shanghai